The Heart Is Big Enough

*For Megan
Michael Rosen
with wishes
for all your
own ♡'s
stories*

MICHAEL J. ROSEN

The Heart Is Big Enough

FIVE STORIES

Harcourt Brace & Company

San Diego   New York   London

Illustrations copyright © 1997 by Matthew Valiquette

Library of Congress Cataloging-in-Publication Data
Rosen, Michael J., 1954–
The heart is big enough: five stories/by Michael J. Rosen.
p.   cm.
Contents: The trust of a dolphin—Juggling—Mastering the
art—The Walkers of Hawthorn Park—The remembering movies.
Summary: In each story a child overcomes a difficult
situation such as a physical disability, parental divorce,
or aging grandparent.
ISBN 0-15-201402-0
1. Courage—Juvenile fiction.   2. Children's stories,
American.   [1. Courage—Fiction.   2. Short stories.]
I. Title.   PZ7.R71868He   1997
[Fic]—dc20   96-22785

Text set in Minion
Designed by Lydia D'moch

First edition
A C E F D B
Printed in the United States of America

Contents

The Heart Is Big Enough

The Trust of a Dolphin

WHEN MATTHEW SWAM, even in the artificially chlorinated, concrete pool at the YMCA, he felt like a dolphin whose home was water. As he propelled himself through water, his body grew sleek, speedy, and powerful as a dolphin's. The goggles made his eyes large as a dolphin's eyes. He could see every tile, Band-Aid, and coin on the pool's bottom. Sometimes Matthew even imagined his body to be a dolphin's sound wave, sent across the water and bouncing off the wall—as he flip-turned—to bring the dolphin news of the world ahead. Since Matthew often had the pool to himself, no one interrupted whatever dolphin story he rehearsed during his swim.

Although his mother had to drive him to and from the swim center and wait while he swam laps or took a private lesson, Matthew had been swimming every other day since the age of three. And now Matthew could swim freestyle, breaststroke, sidestroke, backstroke, and, if he held a kickboard, he could even do the dolphin kick. Probably Matthew could swim better than anyone in his school—even the seventh and eighth graders—but there wasn't a pool at Prairie Middle School.

Matthew dreamed of swimming like a dolphin, but sometimes, on land, just walking, he actually felt like a dolphin whose body, out of water, doesn't work. It felt too heavy. Gravity pulled too hard on his hip and made it ache. That was it: He felt like one of those sad or sick dolphins that strand themselves on the beach and can't swim back into the water—scientists don't understand exactly why it happens... and sometimes can't even save the helpless dolphins.

If Matthew could have been anything in the world besides a human being, he would have been a dolphin. *If Matthew could have been... If Matthew could only...* However often those words were said, Matthew could not, and he knew it. Moreover, the kids in his school knew he couldn't—couldn't run bases, for example. (Someone else could run if Matthew batted the baseball.) Couldn't sit still at his desk. (He *could* get up and walk around without asking the teacher's permission.) Couldn't jump up or hop, couldn't squat down or square-dance (actually, any boy in his class would have been glad to sit out of the square-dancing unit in gym class), couldn't walk home, climb stairs without a hand on the railing, chase some teasing girl and hassling boy (who were always smaller than him); and most of all, Matthew couldn't stand the crutches he had to use when his hip acted up. Probably Matthew would have chosen to be anything at all other than a human being since he could only be a broken one: an eleven-year-old boy with a bad hip the doctors would fix again, once and for all, when Matthew had stopped growing, even though Matthew was already six inches taller than the tallest boy in his homeroom.

His teachers, classmates, doctors, family members—people were always trying to be understanding. And there was one word they always ended up saying, one word Matthew hated: "Matthew, you've been *exceptionally* brave these last few weeks," the mother driving car pool would say, as she helped him into the car. "But for an *exceptionally* determined boy like you...," the school guidance counselor would say. "You've been *exceptionally* patient while we've tried to find you some relief," his doctor's nurse would say. All Matthew heard in their voices was the word *except: Everyone can do this or that except me. That's what* exceptional *means to me,* he thought.

Matthew had never actually seen a dolphin apart from in movies and books. But he had seen every movie. He had read every book. (He could read books his oldest sister was reading in college—she was a freshman. Reading was one thing that didn't bother his hip.) He scanned *TV Guide* each week just to see if there might be a program with oceans or whales or dolphins. He sent his allowance to three different foundations that aided dolphins—to help save them from tuna fishermen and pollutants, of course, but also so he could receive the newsletters: page after page of updates, discoveries, photographs, and unbelievable findings about these mammals that first evolved in water like us people, lived on land for fifty million years like us people, but then returned to water for another fifty million years.

"They're more highly evolved than we are," Matthew often replied when some friend made a crack like, "You've got water on the brain," referring to Matthew's obsession with swimming and dolphins.

It was in the back of *Dolphin Talk,* one newsletter to which Matthew subscribed, that he first saw the ad about a summer camp on Key Largo for teenagers interested in ocean life. The ad describing the two-week camp listed nothing about campfires and tents, archery, horseback riding, Indian lore, or crafts (all the activities offered by the YMCA camp where Matthew was supposed to go that coming summer). In fact, the listing didn't even try to sound fun:

> *Intensive work with Gulf-area marine mammals. Participate in five-year study on human/cetacean interaction. Must be comfortable using snorkel/fins, swimming in water to fifteen feet deep. Limited scholarships available. Twelve interns accepted each summer session. Call toll-free.*

Matthew understood everything about the ad except *interns*; he thought that meant doctors, or almost-doctors.

Marine mammals, of course, meant walrus, manatees, seals and sea lions (which he knew weren't the same thing), whales, and dolphins. *Cetaceans* meant whales and dolphins exclusively. And as for Matthew—Matthew meant to be one of the twelve interns.

"I'd say yes, in a second," his mother replied, when Matthew brought her the ad. "But, kiddo, it says *teenager.*"

"I knew you'd say that. But I'm almost twelve, and I'm bigger than most thirteen-year-olds, aren't I? I'm tall as Claire's friends Ted and Drew, who are in college. So how about if we just call and ask?"

"But you'll be with seventeen- and eighteen-year-olds, too, who will be bigger than you. And not just bigger."

Matthew let his mother pull him toward her for a hug.

"On the other hand," she admitted, "I can't believe any kid would know more than you do about dolphins."

"So I can just tell the people I'm thirteen..."

"Well, then there's the money, Matthew." His mother hated to talk about money, especially money they didn't have. Her face looked as though Matthew had suddenly hurt her feelings. "For two weeks, they charge three times what the Y camp charges for the whole summer. Plus there's the round-trip flight to Florida. You *would* want to come back afterward, wouldn't you?"

"Mom!"

"Well, if you did get a scholarship...and if your father's business does continue to improve—let's hope!—so he could spring for the travel costs, maybe then we could afford it. But I'll mention it to your father next time he calls."

Matthew understood all those reasons, especially the one about money. Since his parents' divorce four years ago, his father's visits and support had lessened instead of increased as he'd promised. They talked more often, and they wrote more letters, but as his father kept saying and writing to Matthew lately, "I just wish my business here in Portland were growing as fast as you are. But don't grow up too much before I see you."

Matthew concluded it wouldn't hurt to call the toll-free number just to speak with someone at the camp.

"Cetacean Research Lab, Roberta Towers," a woman answered.

Matthew stared at the ad he'd already pinned among the changing collage of dolphin material on his bulletin board. "Is this the summer-camp place? I saw your ad?"

"Right. You're speaking of our teen camp—our two-week, 'total immersion' experience—"

"Yes! With dolphins, right?" Matthew interrupted.

"Right...Our program places you directly in the dolphins' environment. How dolphins behave, communicate, echolocate—the ecological problems they face—everything. And you participate firsthand in our ongoing research. We include a half-hour swim every day with one of our two groups of bottlenose dolphins."

Matthew couldn't believe the words the phone had just delivered. "You mean, I'd get to swim out in the ocean with dolphins?"

"Not exactly. Our interns swim with groups of dolphins held in elective captivity, a fenced-in—"

"You have them trapped in some swimming pool?" Matthew interrupted again.

"Perhaps you'd let me finish?" The voice on the other end of the phone had turned icy, like a school principal giving a warning before an assembly. "Concrete, chlorinated pools are contrary to the work we do here. Dolphins must live in the ocean—concrete ruins a dolphin's ability to use sonar: Concrete doesn't absorb the echoes, so everything just bounces back, overloading the dolphin's brain. That kind of captivity separates them from their families, and some never adapt, and they die."

Matthew wanted to hang up, he was so embarrassed. He had read countless times exactly what Roberta had just said. And, of course, he even knew something himself about the problems separations can bring.

"If you're accepted into the program this summer, you'll join the dolphins in their own world. We have an inlet in the Keys where the dolphins *elect* to live. I think that makes our philosophy clear?"

"Sure, I'm sorry," Matthew replied sheepishly. "I just thought when you said 'captivity'—"

"No, I'm sorry for being shrill, but we get swamped with calls from people looking for an aquatic petting zoo—and that kind of exploitation gives our research a bad name."

"I understand—I want to be a part of your real program..."

"I assume you are a competent swimmer; that is a prerequisite."

"I can swim every stroke," Matthew answered. "I swim a mile in twenty-nine minutes, ten seconds—I can do half a mile of just dolphin kicks. You don't have to do the combined butterfly stroke perfectly...or do you?"

Matthew's quick response made Roberta laugh. "Quite honestly," she said, "if you can use flippers and a snorkel, you'll be fine."

"No problem," Matthew said, and since that was a lie, another followed it without any trouble. "And is thirteen old enough to come?"

"Sure, that's the cutoff—thirteen through eighteen. It would help if you're a thirteen-year-old who's a little familiar with ocean life. It's really a college-level course we're offering."

"I know a lot, really—not just for my age. My teachers at school even think so." Matthew could hardly believe the words that he, Matthew, was saying over the telephone: He never had the chance to brag—not at school, not to his older sisters, not to his father. And here he was, bragging, first about his swimming ability and then about his dolphin knowledge, which no one, not even his family, really shared.

After Matthew posed several other questions about their resident dolphins, he finally inquired about money. "And what if, say, a person doesn't have enough money, right now, and maybe needs a scholarship?"

Roberta promised to send Matthew a scholarship application, a camp brochure, and a newsletter about their ongoing research. "Call back if you have more questions," Roberta said. "Hope to see you this summer. You sound like you're motivated, which is what we want."

Matthew was so excited when he hung up the phone, he could have leaped into the air from his chair, if only his hip were willing. Instead, he shuffled from the room, shouting, "Mom! Claire! Lou Anne!" forgetting that his mother and sisters had gone to the Laundromat.

Was it still a lie, he wondered, if telling it only made something good happen?

The teen camp information arrived on Matthew's twelfth birthday. He spent all the afternoon filling out the application. Only one question perplexed him: *What personal goal do you hope to accomplish with this internship? Attach as many sheets as you want.*

"All that means is," Claire explained, "why do you want

to go? Just send them a picture of your room—they'll see you're a bigger dolphin nutcase than they are."

It was true. Matthew had plastered his walls with color maps of the ocean, charts of dolphin species, and a poster illustrating the life of a bottlenose dolphin. A mobile of paper dolphins leaped above his saltwater fish tank. The books on his shelves, the bookends, the paperweight—all dolphins.But no photograph of a kid's room would win him a scholarship.

By dinnertime, when friends and relatives had gathered for a cookout, Matthew had composed twelve pages of reasons why he wanted to learn about dolphins, swim with dolphins, communicate with dolphins. Of course, not one of the reasons happened to allude to his hip and how his body made him feel like a dolphin, in and out of the water. (But since his hip problem wouldn't interfere with his swimming at the camp, this wasn't another lie, he figured.)

"Mom, you have to sign the camp application, too," he said, presenting the completed form. "You're my guardian."

"I thought I was just your mom. OK, get a pen, but promise me you won't be too disappointed if the scholarship doesn't come through—"

"I'll understand," Matthew said. "I'll go to the Y camp, like we planned."

"Your father also mentioned to me—I don't think he'd mind my telling you, since it is your birthday—that if things don't work out, maybe you could spend a couple weeks with him in Portland."

"That'd be great!" Matthew exclaimed. "But what would be greater is going to Key Largo and then to Portland—"

"And after that, to the moon," Claire added, with a poke in Matthew's ribs.

The only present Matthew really wanted he received: His mother and sisters gave him a professional snorkel and mask, and a pair of fins. "And don't bother asking, Matthew," his mother said, anticipating Matthew's very thought. "I can't run you to the swim center in the middle of your own birthday party."

But the next day and every day (not every other day) thereafter, Matthew practiced with his new equipment. Summer was months away. The scholarship might never arrive. Nonetheless, Matthew set his mind and body to mastering the snorkeling gear.

At first Matthew swallowed water when the tip of the snorkel dipped below the surface. The flippers made his calves sore, and sometimes, he hated to admit, they made his hip throb. But within a few weeks, he could swim a mile using it all—in half the time of his usual mile. He learned to dive to the bottom of the swim center's twelve-foot diving well, pinching his nose and forcing his breath against his eardrums to relieve the pressure. (*Dolphins can dive deeper than five hundred feet,* he recited to himself.) With the added fin power, Matthew experimented with all kinds of dolphin maneuvers: He spiraled through the water...flutter-kicked in backward circles...somersaulted...flapped his flippers together on the surface, the way a dolphin smacks its tail to show anger... He jumped from the deep-end floor and kicked to the surface, spouting water from his snorkel as if it were his blowhole.

By the time Matthew could swim the entire length of the pool underwater in one held breath, he had received the official letter: He had been awarded a scholarship for the second summer session of what he'd started calling dolphin camp. The expectation of those fourteen days in the middle of summer buoyed Matthew through the rest of the school year: through recesses and gym periods; through hours of track and soccer; the Christmas vacation of ice-skating; the winter of trampoline, wrestling, and relay races; the warming days of volleyball and kickball and all the other sports that he watched in his role as referee or official timer or halfhearted player. Nothing else bothered Matthew. Nothing else mattered to Matthew. He simply and happily lived within his routine of swimming laps after school and reading dolphin books at night. (School became something that passed the time until summer.) He clocked himself at faster speeds than he had ever swum before. And as for his reading, by May there wasn't a book in the catalog of the public library under the words *dolphin, cetacean,* or *oceanography* that he hadn't studied from cover to cover.

"Did you know that some scientists think dolphins can stun fish by making a web of very loud sound waves—and then just eat them up?" Matthew loved sharing the facts he discovered. "Dolphins need fresh water to drink, like we do. But they can't drink salt water, either, so know how they get it? Come on, guess! From the bodies of the fish they eat."

Even though some people tried to be especially nice or patient or tolerant on account of Matthew's hip, even Claire and Lou Anne and his closest friends at school were bored of dolphindolphindolphin talk. "The camp counselors are supposed to be the experts, not the campers!" Lou Anne reminded him. "That's why you're going there instead of them coming here."

"That's a great idea—let's call and see if they can come up here with the dolphins," Matthew said; he could be as big a smart aleck as his sister.

Only twice since Matthew received the scholarship and the plane tickets (a surprise Valentine's Day present from his father) did he need to use his crutches.

The first was a two-week stretch in the spring, playing full-court-press basketball (which he didn't even want to play, but practically the entire neighborhood was chanting his name because there weren't enough kids to even up the sides). The ache in his hip required a visit to his bone doctor, painkillers, heating pads, elevation, and crutches—just so he could sleep at night and walk short distances during the day.

And the second time he needed the crutches—two days before his flight to Key Largo. Matthew had awakened with such stiffness in his hip and back that he could barely bend down to do the stretches that were supposed to keep his hip from hurting.

"It's probably just excitement—being anxious," Dr. Oshofsky diagnosed. "A kind of overall tensing up could have triggered it." But Matthew knew that the pain in his hip didn't need something to trigger it. It sometimes hurt just because his body was growing, just because gravity pulled.

"Why is it, when you want something really bad, just wanting it keeps you from getting it?" Matthew said, leaving the examining room, his mother trying to catch up with his impatient hobbling steps.

"I think I understand what you're saying, but..."

"You know. Just because I really wanted my hip not to hurt now, now is when it's hurting—forget it. Let's just get in the car."

The day of his departure, Matthew boarded the crowded airliner early, along with the elderly people and the babies. Though he didn't know anyone waiting at the gate, he knew everyone was watching him: *What happened to that tall kid on crutches?* Matthew had an aisle seat at the very back, where he could keep his stiff leg outstretched. The whole trip the flight attendants had to step carefully around him.

The painkillers stopped the sharp pains but not the aching. Ache was a reminder that if he didn't take it easy, didn't use his crutches, and didn't rest his hip, then real pain would return—maybe worse. Ache was like someone calling his name all the time, taunting him, and Matthew could do almost nothing to stop it. (And just as with some kinds of teasing, the same advice applied: Try to ignore it.)

After two long flights and a two-hour drive in the research center van, Matthew arrived at the bay where he would spend the two weeks he had been awaiting for nearly thirty-two weeks. All that sitting in one position increased the ache in his hip, and he swallowed the optional painkillers—true, they didn't act instantly—before he walked into the research center office to check in.

The camp had no counselors. There were only the four staff members of the Key Largo Cetacean Research Lab: Consuelo, who first gathered the dozen dolphins and directed the lab with her husband, Paul, an oceanographer; Art, who was finishing his doctoral work as a marine biologist; and Kingsley, a white-haired British scientist who had been studying dolphin communication for fifty years. Matthew had hoped to meet Roberta, the woman he'd spoken with on the phone, but she had research in New England that month.

Students from the local colleges worked part-time for the

center, and other people were employed in the office, the computer labs, or the kitchen. But no counselor took charge of the twelve teenagers (eleven, plus Matthew) who were to bunk, four to a cabin, during the next two weeks. After a woman named Rita registered Matthew and issued his locker key, field notebooks, and research folders, Matthew glanced at the first page of his two-week schedule:

DAY ONE

10–5:00	*Intern arrival, check-in, cabin assignments*
5:00	*Orientation (bayside shelter)*
6:00	*Barbecue supper (picnic tables)*
7:30	*General philosophy of Center, overview*

He was on his own for the next three hours, until five.

Straining to walk as though his hip weren't bothering him, Matthew left the office. Outside he pushed open the huge gates of an enclosing wooden fence and entered the research grounds. In a single instant, months of waiting, years of fantasizing, and nights of only dreaming—all that ended, and culminated in one glance: The tip of a dorsal fin broke the surface of the water not ten yards from him. Another fin. A sound that was unmistakable yet altogether surprising. And then the large silver-gray head of a dolphin lolled at the surface with one eye gazing up, looking--no, *watching* Matthew. From under the water, the dolphin had sensed that someone, that Matthew, had entered the compound.

Nothing but a stone walkway spread between Matthew and the water. The air crackled with the dolphins' clicking, the chopping of the waves, the flapping of a cormorant's wings too soggy to lift the large bird from the salty water.

Across the narrow channel that stretched between the Atlantic Ocean and the Gulf of Mexico, chain-link fences cut the seawater into three sections: two dolphin areas and a narrower channel in the middle where small boats could pass. A few buildings, three thatched shelters, tropical plants and trees that Matthew had seen only in photographs, a wooden privacy fence...and dolphins. And nothing else. Nothing that remotely resembled any other summer camp.

Matthew nearly forgot about the crutches that he had stowed behind some prickly bushes outside the office door. He retrieved them, carried his backpack and suitcase to the first cabin, unloaded everything on one of the two lower bunks (no one else had arrived yet), spread sunscreen over all his exposed skin, and returned to the water's edge, where he remained for the rest of the afternoon.

All the facts he had read, all the pictures he had studied, all the sounds he had heard recorded with underwater microphones for television—all that vanished like the shadows that cease to exist as soon as a light switch is flipped. Suddenly everything was exposed in bright natural light: live, real, and not made for an audience or a camera but for Matthew alone. And the smell—he had forgotten to expect that: brine, cedar, a sweetness like pineapple...but those weren't the exact odor. Matthew couldn't define it. The smell was just steamy, salty, citrus, maybe sweet like cinnamon—it was something for which Matthew found no vocabulary.

And the dolphins, they were bigger—no, not bigger than he thought they'd be; but their three, four, five hundred pounds looked more lifelike—they weren't *like* life, they *were* life! The dolphins Matthew had pictured before were nothing more than printer's ink and videotape and imagined details. Someone else's experience. And these—one...two...six dolphins were breathing, spouting; watchful animals gliding and cavorting in the clear almost gold water that was their home.

The dolphins circled and dove, sometimes popping up right next to the edge where Matthew stood. As one streamed past, an eye peered directly at Matthew. *Dolphins see as well in the water as out of the water,* Matthew remembered. He even recalled an article about the dolphins in one of the first sea aquaria that had taken to throwing pebbles from their pool directly at some nuns in the audience. Their aim was incredible. The nuns' black habits reminded the dolphins of their rivals, the sea lions. And now—now!—instead of Matthew studying some library book about dolphins, the dolphins were studying him.

As Matthew met each camper—intern, rather—who arrived, the years that Matthew had hoped would add to his age slowly disappeared, month by month. He had never felt more underage in his life. He wasn't even a seventh grader yet, and each person who was introduced looked not only older but more—what was the word?—*experienced? qualified? confident?* As with the smell of the water, Matthew couldn't name his feelings about all these teenagers. (Or maybe it was the feeling of trying to figure out the feelings he was supposed to be feeling as a teenager.) No, no one looked thirteen, or even fourteen.

Of the twelve interns, Matthew would come to know best:

Rosetta and Arlen, who had spent the previous summer at the research center camp. They had come from Seattle, Washington: "From the northwest tip of America to the southeast tip," Arlen said, describing their overnight flight.

Lee, who had logged in sixty hours scuba diving—not just snorkeling but using oxygen tanks on the ocean floor!

Twins named Stephen and Lydia, who had both tried out for the U.S. Olympic swim team. Matthew didn't even want to know how fast they could swim a mile.

If it weren't for his sisters' talk about high school and freshman year, Matthew wouldn't even have known some of the things his fellow interns were talking about. When he did understand the topic—for instance, Matthew knew that SATs and ACTs were tests that high school kids needed to get into college—he had nothing to contribute.

Not one of the other interns was misled by Matthew's size: However tall and broad he was for his age, he was the youngest kid there. Not that anyone had said anything mean or condescending to Matthew, it was just that no one had said much of anything directly to him. They could just look at Matthew, as though they were looking inside him, and tell that he was too young. Matthew thought that maybe they felt he was like someone's kid brother they were stuck with for their whole vacation.

The first night everyone at the center shared a barbecue supper in a thatched shelter that bordered the dolphins' pool. Though there wasn't an actual lecture scheduled, some of the interns gathered around Rosetta. "So if the dolphins are free to leave if they want, why are there fences?" Lydia asked.

"To keep out other things," Rosetta answered. "Any one of these dolphins can leap an eight-foot fence without even concentrating."

Matthew looked across the yard at the chain-link partitions, and then at the water, where a jagged series of dorsal fins flowed across the moonlit surface like a kid's illustration of waves.

"Once a week the fence gates are opened and the dolphins swim out into the ocean," Rosetta continued. "They hang out a few hours or a day—sometimes longer, I guess—and then they come back. They always have. For six years."

"But why?" Lee asked. "Do they really prefer swimming with people?"

Art brought a platter of cut-up pineapples to the table

and supplied an answer. "The dolphins know they've got a good, dependable food source right here. And they're protective of it. So they return. I also happen to think we people amuse them."

"There we are, bobbing around on the surface in our silly masks and pretend flippers," said Arlen, "so we've got to look like a bunch of Halloween clowns to them."

"Or some trained act at Sea World: The Amazing High School Humans," Art added.

DAY TWO
8:00   *Breakfast*
9:00   *Bay ecology, habitats; begin species inventory*
12:00   *Lunch, free time*
2:00   *Dolphin interaction period #1*

All morning Matthew hiked the shorelines with the other interns and Art, the marine biologist. They created a day's list for each shorebird, geological specimen, plant species, and invertebrate they encountered. Some interns used sketchbooks, some cameras, some charts and rulers, some binoculars. Eventually they traded equipment. Matthew wrote notes, gathered samples, took measurements, and walked and walked and walked, until each step made him wince. (He hadn't brought the crutches—what good would they have done on sand or on rocky shores?)

Art recited so many phenomenal facts and statistics—so much that Matthew had never even read about. Between recording in his notebooks what he didn't want to forget and struggling to walk without a limp, Matthew could barely keep up. His head reeled with questions.

"...salt count here is so high, you'll find it much harder to dive."

Matthew had missed some of what Art was saying. *Why should diving be a problem?* he wondered, but he didn't ask another question.

By afternoon, when Matthew sat on the picnic tables, preparing for his first swim with the dolphins, he realized that he was afraid. Not afraid of dolphins. Not afraid of swimming in the ocean for the first time in his life. Afraid of the pain in his hip. The medicine hadn't relieved the throbbing from the morning hike. Here he was at the dolphin center on Key Largo, ten feet away from a group of six bottlenose dolphins, wondering if he should remain on shore.

"The main thing to remember," Consuelo began, "is not to be disappointed. You're making contact with a foreign, alien, other intelligence. Contact is something you must develop. It's rarely immediate. You might think the dolphins are being standoffish or distant. Yes, they're curious, but they're also cautious. They might avoid you at first. Hey, if I were a dolphin, I might avoid meeting myself, if I didn't know any better."

The new interns looked at each other's puzzled faces, as if to say, *Why did we pay all this money if we aren't really going to have these so-called interactions?*

"Think of yourself as a guest," she continued. "You are entering the dolphins' home. You are the stranger, the unknown, the one who might cause harm. So everything you do should work toward winning the dolphins' trust. Think of these rules as dolphin etiquette."

Somehow Matthew had never thought there would be rules. *Isn't swimming with dolphins just swimming?*

"First thing: Don't use your hands. No paddling, no swimming strokes of any kind, no treading water, reaching, grabbing, and so on. Got it? That's unnerving to dolphins— they don't have hands, so hands are not something they can predict. Keep your hands alongside your body. If you don't follow this rule, they'll most likely avoid you and swim with someone else. Any questions?"

No questions. Just lots of concerned expressions.

"Second thing: Dolphins are horizontal creatures; we're vertical creatures. So convert to a dolphin's orientation: Stay horizontal. Float, kick, but don't tread water or just 'stand' upright in the water. The dolphins assume a vertical position means you're in distress—that you're wounded or sick—and they'll often prod you into the 'right,' horizontal position."

Matthew had never dreamed in his dreams of swimming with dolphins, had never considered in his hours of swim or snorkel practice that his arms would be threatening, that his hands could be dangerous. He wasn't a harpoon. He didn't mean harm. But now, when his hip pained him more than he could remember since his last surgery, now he had to swim without his arms.

"Third: Dolphins greet each other side to side; they see best directly to the side—that's where their eyes are. They move their heads from side to side to make out what's ahead. So don't swim up to a dolphin head-on. Swim alongside and make eye contact. That's very important—look... how can

I say it?—look *trustingly* into the eye that's greeting you."

Consuelo spoke slowly and carefully, but Matthew felt woozy with all this new information that jumbled together with his own thoughts and recollections as well as his own body's warnings.

"What number am I on? Let's say it's five: Don't touch a dolphin unless a dolphin touches you first. They must initiate contact. For instance, they might decide to rub against the back of your knees—that's trusting and friendly."

Everyone had questions, even though everyone wished the lecture were over so they could start the swim. Consuelo's rules continued. "Remember the dolphin is a dominant creature. That's a little switch for our human egos, I know. But in the water, they are the powerful and controlling intelligence. So they'll want to check you out. You'll feel their sonar all around you. If it's right next to you, you might feel a little vibration, like static electricity."

Consuelo took a sip from a water bottle. "Oh, and one might even want to taste you."

All the interns laughed at this idea. "I thought you fed them herring, not people," Lee joked.

"No, people we feed to the sharks," Consuelo joked in

reply. "Seriously, dolphins have lost their sense of smell, but taste helps them identify you. So don't be alarmed if you see a dolphin opening its mouth around your leg or arm. They have teeth, of course, but they'll just press their taste buds against you. Don't jerk away, though—you could pull against the teeth, which are sharp."

Consuelo passed a clipboard to each intern. On it a grid listed a wide range of "human/dolphin" interactions. Each person had to complete the form after each swim, logging the nature and approximate duration of each contact he or she had experienced with each dolphin. There were spaces labeled *eye contact, parallel swimming, touching, mouthing, dorsal tow,* and many other things Matthew didn't believe that Consuelo had explained yet.

"Last of all," Consuelo said, "let's call this Consuelo's golden rule: Remember that dolphins are not only interesting but they're interested creatures. Besides being open to their ways of behaving, and besides being careful and respectful, each of you has to be interesting. Fun. Playful. Try diving, making noises, tossing their toys, using a kickboard, creating group waves. So open your eyes and your ears as well as your hearts, and see what the dolphins might suggest. And remember, don't be disappointed. And there's no reason to be nervous, either. Sometimes they'll pick you out as simpatico—a friend—and sometimes they're not sure. Give them time. Dolphin personalities are as various as human personalities—not everyone's an outgoing party animal."

"Speak for yourself, Consuelo," her husband, Paul, called from the sidelines.

"Now, the ladies here have a slightly better chance: Dolphins find children least threatening and most interesting, then females, and—sorry, guys—we've found that they're a little more cautious with men."

As Matthew spit and rubbed his saliva in his mask to keep it from fogging, Paul, who had never spoken directly with Matthew, crouched beside him on the floating dock. "I gather the crutches leaning against the wall are yours, right?"

"Yeah, but I don't need them, really."

"I see. And you can swim without any difficulty?"

"A mile in twenty-nine minutes—half that with flippers." Matthew spoke with as much confidence as his nervousness would allow. "But that's using my arms, of course. I'm sort of used to using my arms—except when I use a flutterboard. I'm also sort of used to swimming-pool water."

"Well, this is how and where the dolphins swim, so you get to meet them on their terms. You'll get used to it. Plenty of swims ahead. Don't push yourself."

Don't push yourself. Matthew had heard that advice before...about a thousand times before...but it was almost comforting that this stranger would offer Matthew those same words.

The interns had divided into two groups; half went to swim on the far side of the channel with the other dolphin group. In Matthew's pool, the one male dolphin was named Kingpin; the five females were named Queenie, Princess, Jester, T. P. (for Tiny Princess), and Tulip (who used to swim in the other group but had constantly fought with Daisy, so she'd had to trade places with Regina).

Even before Matthew had pulled on his flippers (his right leg wouldn't bend so easily), the tallest intern, Stephen, the Olympic swimmer, slid into the water, a belt of scuba-diving weights encircling his waist. No one had told Matthew to bring weights.

Rosetta flopped in next. "Wait till you see the tricks I've cooked up—they're going to love swimming with me!" she said, and jingled her cupped palms by Matthew's ear.

"Pennies—they love the jingling." Rosetta plugged the snorkel in her mouth and dove.

As Matthew lowered his legs into the water, he saw the blur of a dolphin darting beneath his feet. Inches away. *Why didn't anyone tell me to bring diving weights, or pennies, even?* he wondered. *Why didn't someone say you don't use your arms—I could have practiced.*

The water was warmer than he expected. Matthew eased himself slowly under the surface. As soon as his ears submerged, he heard the *clickclickclick* of the dolphin sonar, loud and close and everywhere at once. Even before Matthew could shift into the correct horizontal, nonthreatening, floating position—even before he had shot the in-rushing salt water from his snorkel—a dolphin raced over to Matthew's body, touched its rostrum to his side, and sent a burst of prickling sound waves through his skin. It didn't hurt, but it so startled Matthew (it was so immediate, unexpected, thrilling—where were the words!) that he gasped, inhaled instead of expelled the water from his snorkel, and gulped a salty mouthful. Abruptly his arms thrashed through the water, his legs kicked him into a vertical position, and Matthew emerged at the surface choking. It was Paul who reached for his hand and tugged Matthew onto the dock he'd left not ten seconds before.

"You're OK. Here, you're fine," Paul said. "Wow, take a couple breaths. Looks like Queenie wanted to meet you right away."

The two interns just climbing into the water didn't say anything. They didn't need to—Matthew could guess what everyone who'd just witnessed this was thinking; it was what the kids in school always thought when his hip made him stumble or when he retired from a game to sit out-of-bounds in two chairs, one for propping up his leg.

Once Matthew had removed his gear and assured Paul and the other adults who rushed over that he was fine, they posed all the questions they had been gathering since his arrival.

"Is it your leg?"

"Are you sure you should be swimming?"

"Did this problem just develop?"

"Should we call your parents?"

Matthew could barely hear the volley of questions—he already knew those, too. Their words sailed over his head like balls he didn't have a chance of catching and wasn't about to chase just trying to look good. All he focused on was the feeling of the dolphin's echo on his skin.

Finally Paul's suggestion grabbed his attention: "Maybe today is a good day to just observe the other swimmers, and tomorrow you can do two swims if you're feeling up to it."

"But—" Now Matthew wanted to answer their questions—he even thought he could answer them honestly. *It was an accident,* he wanted to explain, *I was just startled before I'd even*—but Paul had already handed him a clipboard. "You help me do the shore observations today."

And so Matthew watched instead of swam for the half hour. *Now, even with swimming, I'm sitting out,* Matthew chided himself.

The first thing Matthew observed was how well the other interns could dive, how long they could hold their breaths. (Longer than he could? Stephen certainly could.) Lee's flippers sped him across the water as if he were racing instead of just snorkeling. (But then, Matthew remembered that he'd never seen his own body propelled by flippers.) The dolphins surfaced here and there, trailed this person, dodged that person, swerved by in pairs. As far as he could see, no dolphin had touched anyone yet. No intern had been tasted.

(Matthew wasn't sure he wanted to be tasted.) He could see the whole pod circulating beneath and beside and above the five—instead of six—swimmers.

Paul suggested ways that Matthew could recognize each dolphin by identifying marks on the back, tail, and dorsal fin. "Dolphins know one another by their signature sounds—everyone has a different, let's say, voice. But since we're a little slow at picking up those bursts of sound, it's easier for us to notice cuts and scratches and notches."

When Paul began to describe Queenie's markings, the narrower pitch of her dorsal fin, the dark streak behind her blowhole, Matthew asked, "You know, when I entered the water, Queenie—you said it was?—came right over and buzzed me with echoes so my side tingled. She came so close to me, and so soon? I thought—"

"Well, sonar is how a dolphin reads you. If you tense your muscles, which people do when they're nervous, the dolphin's sonar can sense that—they'll know you're frightened or—"

"Oh, but I wasn't scared at all," Matthew insisted, which was true. "My muscles weren't tensed, I don't think."

"No, I believe you. Well, maybe Queenie's sonar told her

something else about you," Paul replied. "Sometimes I think dolphins can tell more about us than we can know ourselves. It's just that they can't tell us what they're knowing. *So far.*"

There was no scheduled bedtime or lights-out at the research camp. After the evening swim, everyone gathered in a large room behind the lab office to watch a documentary film about the rescuing of two pilot whales who had stranded themselves on the Keys. Consuelo, Paul, and most of the other staff Matthew had met at the center were among the people who had struggled around the clock for two days in the emergency. Without water to buoy them, the whales' own weight, pulled by gravity, was crushing their own inner organs. The rescuers kept the whales wet so they didn't dry out; they applied gallons of sunscreen to prevent them from getting sunburned; they performed medical checkups every two hours; and finally the boats they arranged for towed the huge creatures into deeper water. This rescue was successful, but Matthew had read about many that were not.

But before, after, and even during the film, all the interns talked about was their first dolphin swim.

"The pennies really worked, at first."

"I think the dolphins on our side weren't in a good mood. They just swam around, not very close."

"One almost rubbed across my knees, just when it was time to get out."

"I slid my hand along the side of one, but then it bolted away. I blew it."

"For a long while I just swam right between two of them."

"Wasn't it like meeting a creature from another planet— one that's completely underwater?"

"Do they really get to know us?" someone asked Rosetta, who had, in a short time, become the unofficial expert.

"You'll just have to wait and see. I shouldn't ruin any possible surprises. But the dolphins know we're here for a while; things will happen."

Then Arlen, the other returning intern, reported on her swim with the dolphin pod Matthew didn't observe. "I remembered Daisy from last year, maybe she remembered me—we spent the whole time together. Just looking at each other. I got to rub her skin, and she wriggled a few times over my legs. She even tasted me on my ankle, I think. It was pretty quick, but I think she thought I tasted friendly."

"And just how does 'friendly' taste, Arlen?" Lee asked.

Even without a story of his own to share, Matthew was engulfed by the others' excitement. A few interns sounded jealous of Arlen's lucky swim. A few seemed so eager for the next swim that Matthew wondered what would keep them from jumping into the water right then, at ten-thirty at night.

Some interns obviously intended to compare stories all night; two others headed for the door, so Matthew joined them and returned to his cabin. If nothing else, he could take the painkillers, stretch out his leg, and hope that his hip would be better for the next day. Hope seemed as effective as anything else, since really all hope is, is time, more time.

As soon as Matthew lay on his bed, the tears started. It wasn't the pain in his hip; he was used to that (though often it did make him cry). It wasn't being away from home and it wasn't fear of the older interns making fun of him or even ignoring him. And it certainly wasn't fear of the water or the dolphins. He couldn't say why he was upset. It was as though, ever since he arrived, he had lost whatever power of speech he had possessed. And yet gravity didn't harm him the way it almost killed those stranded pilot whales. The way it killed lots of dolphins and whales that couldn't be rescued. But

maybe it was the fact that Matthew might not be able to...
that Matthew couldn't—well, just *couldn't*. Was it just too
much for a twelve-year-old boy with a partly plastic hip (that
had to be acting up right now!) to think he could remember
Consuelo's zillion rules and swim without using his arms in
a saltwater channel with a group of bottlenose dolphins?

Matthew climbed out of bed again, pulled on a pair of
shorts and a sweatshirt, and left the cabin in case his crying
got louder or his cabinmates returned.

On crutches just to help his hip relax for tomorrow's
swim—*swims*, he hoped—Matthew walked around the bay
where the dolphins were sleeping. Four dorsal fins broke the
surface, then one sank and another rose to the top, a blowhole
releasing a jet of air and spray. Matthew could see the open
eye of the dolphin nearest to him—the bright fleck of the
moon reflected on it. He had read how dolphins sleep: He
knew that the dolphin's other eye was closed so that one
entire half of its brain could almost shut down to rest. The
watchful eye and its half of the brain kept the dolphin sur-
facing to breathe, guarding against danger, looking for the
other dolphins. Then the sides would switch jobs, so the other
half could rest.

Matthew dropped his crutches in the grass and lay across the concrete still cooling from the day's sun. The heat seeped into his hip, and he flattened his body against it as though it were a blanket that would keep him warm. The shushing of the blowholes, the slapslapping of the current, the hum of the center's generators, the whooshing of the breeze in the palm fronds . . . all these sounds lulled Matthew to sleep beside the cycling dolphins—*real* dolphins, not just the mobile of paper ones jangling in his bedroom back home.

DAY THREE
8:00   Breakfast
9:00   Dolphin communication basics (Kingsley Croft)
10:30   Dolphin interaction period #2

Though Matthew's stomach filled with eggs and toast, and his notebook filled with astonishing facts about dolphin language (proving that he had, in fact, sat through breakfast and the first lecture), Matthew concentrated on nothing but the upcoming swim. His medication hadn't worked overnight, and though they didn't have another early-morning hike, his hip throbbed its constant reminder.

Consuelo offered no further advice at the start of this session, so the interns quickly donned their gear and climbed onto the dock. It happened all too fast. The interns were in the water almost before Matthew had worked his legs out from underneath the picnic table. *Listen to your body,* Matthew repeated the doctors' words to himself, *it's telling you something.* "And I'm telling it to shut up," Matthew replied out loud, then marched toward the floating dock.

"I'm going to...um, just help observe today, if that's OK," Matthew said to Paul, who had already started making marks on his clipboard.

"There's nothing we can do to help?" Paul asked.

Matthew managed to keep from crying, but he knew Paul could tell that he was on the verge of tears. And so he was for the whole half hour of his second dolphin swim, as the check marks covered his ledger along with the drips of salt water—from the splashing of the dolphins, *not* from his eyes.

As mysteriously as Matthew's hip had begun hurting, the next morning it began feeling better. At least the pain didn't scare him so much. Matthew knew he could swim this time. (Even if his hip had been worse, Matthew would have swum.)

This time Matthew entered the water as though he were climbing into bed—one foot under the surface...the other foot...then his back, shoulders, head. He held his breath as he turned himself facedown, cleared his snorkel, and began a slow flutter-kick, his hands tucked into his armpits to imitate pectoral fins.

Instantly he could see the dolphins blurring past him, circling the other interns, diving toward the yellow-green bottom of the inlet. The crackling sound of the echoes filled the water, some loud and close, some soft and farther away. Matthew turned his mask left and right—the dolphins swam like...like water in water: a solid body of faster water rushing through the standing-still water. Their bodies plummeted and pivoted, whipped and pirouetted, veered toward and away and then back toward Matthew. *Their bodies are nothing like ours,* Matthew thought, *no matter how well a person can swim.*

Suddenly an eye came alongside Matthew's—not two inches away—and a body slid beneath him, turned instantly, and glided back. Was it Queenie again, or another dolphin? Simultaneously Matthew could feel—or was it hear?—the clicking echoes enter his body. Then there was no mistaking the sensation. The dolphin pushed its rostrum directly against his right side and slid it like a stethoscope down his body and along his leg... and then, with a few powerful whips of the tail, vanished.

Matthew lifted his head above the water. The other interns floated here and there, spread out across the whole inlet. A dorsal fin, a slapping tail, passed someone. A dolphin bounced a rubber ball with its nose. Consuelo shouted to someone, "Don't tread water!"

The crackling, tingling, prodding returned at Matthew's side. He dropped his face into the water. There were two dolphins! Both nudged his side, both sent sound waves through his body. Then one skimmed her belly across his legs. Her skin was sandpapery—Very Fine sandpaper. She turned her white belly alongside Matthew and pressed beside him. Her one eye stared into Matthew's eyes. He opened his eyes wide, and then wider.

"Matthew! Matthew!" He could hear his name being called above the surface. It was Consuelo's voice. "Go ahead, that's Queenie, go ahead, make contact. Touch her—behind her head, on her side."

Matthew dropped his mask under the water again. There

was Queenie, looking as though she were listening to Consuelo, too, waiting for advice about her role in the encounter. Matthew reached his hand toward her, palming the light zigzag of another dolphin's teeth marks on her side. He smiled. He widened his eyes—not because it made him see more but so Queenie would know, he hoped, that she could trust him. And then she circled again so she could prod Matthew's waist. Once again she darted off, her tail flipping an inch—it couldn't have been more!—from Matthew's face. His heart beat so fast from the excitement he could hear the sound in his eardrums. Maybe Queenie could read his heartbeat or his brain waves—maybe she knew about his dolphin dreams, his dolphin swims.

Before he even tried to follow, Queenie raced back to him. Two other dolphins swam at her side. All three circled his body, all three sent their echoes clicking furiously around his waist. And then Matthew realized: *They know about my hip. They can tell.*

Consuelo had run around the inlet to stand on the shore nearest Matthew. "Swim over here. They've found something fascinating about you." As Matthew kicked toward Consuelo, he counted all six dolphins beneath him. The entire group swirled, dove, circled below his body—he was a part of their community.

"Keep swimming, don't come out, you're doing great! I just want to tell you—well, ask you. They've focused on your waist, right? Is there any..."

Matthew floated on his back so he could remain horizontal and talk. But what was he going to say? The truth? The dolphins knew it. But if the humans—if the center staff knew it, wouldn't they send him home: a fake teenager with a fake hip? They wouldn't want the responsibility or the risk; he'd heard that many times before. And if he told another lie? The dolphins would expose him.

Matthew could feel their sonar against his back. Another dolphin grinned in the water beside his head. Finally Matthew admitted, "My hip. It's partly plastic, but that doesn't mean I can't—"

"Well, that's interesting to them. They know that's not usual, because they've swum with lots of people," Consuelo called. "They're intrigued! They're fascinated by exceptional features. They'll all want to swim with you."

Matthew couldn't believe what he was hearing. If he had any doubts about Consuelo's reaction to his news, her smile, broad as a dolphin's, assured him that he wouldn't be leaving. "Choose one dolphin to really connect with—they can be jealous about their playmates. Why not Queenie, since she discovered you? Which is really rare for her—she doesn't usually choose friends. She's the one with the notch at the base of her dorsal fin—bobbing right next to you."

Matthew flutter-kicked away from the shore. Queenie remained at his side, nudging, clicking, staring. She nuzzled him again at his hip, and Matthew reached toward her side and stroked her—her back, her side. And then Queenie turned and slid her body across his knees, back and forth. Four, five times.

Matthew could hear Consuelo calling him again just as Queenie swam again to his side, her eye peering right into his. He lifted his head to hear Consuelo's words, and Queenie dove, returning again to the same position at his side.

"This is remarkable—she's offering you a tow. Take her dorsal fin with your left hand, thumb down. Grab hold firmly. She'll tow you, maybe dive. You'll be fine. Don't be scared—but it can be fast."

As soon as Matthew's hand grasped Queenie's dorsal fin, he could tell that Consuelo had guessed right. The dolphin's tail propelled the two of them across the surface. Water rushed against Matthew's mask, blurring the other dolphins that swam past, the other interns that floated by. Swimming under Queenie's power was nothing like the boost of his swim fins, nothing like a sprint; no, this was blasting through water. The ocean rushing across his body tugged, sucked, scrubbed his skin, as though it were removing his human awkwardness and changing him, transforming him into something more streamlined than a human. They sped from one side of the inlet to the other in seconds. Matthew had never swum this fast, and he knew Queenie was hardly moving at a dolphin's easy twenty miles an hour. (By himself, Matthew could swim, maybe, two miles an hour.)

And then—Matthew couldn't say how—he sensed that Queenie wanted to dive with him. He sucked in a large breath through his snorkel and held it deep in his lungs. And then, somehow, Queenie sensed that Matthew was ready, and she dove toward the ocean floor. Beneath his feet Matthew could feel Queenie's tail forcing water up and down. Other dolphins swooped across their path, watching, eyes wide-open and enormous! Matthew saw another intern waving toward him from below the dock. But just as Matthew felt the need for another breath, Queenie shot to the surface. *She knows when I need to breathe*, Matthew thought.

Again Queenie towed Matthew across the waves, faster this time. All Matthew could see—feel, rather—was the spray of water and bubbles against his mask; but sight didn't matter. All that mattered was the sensation of cutting through the water—of being a living jet of water gushing through the ocean. With the dolphin's fin in his hand, Matthew's human body forgot itself. He moved with the dolphin like a dolphin. Gravity and pain and plastic and bone had all been stranded behind him on the shore.

When Queenie's fin slipped from Matthew's grip, she halted almost instantly, flipped back upon herself in a tight about-face, paused for Matthew to grab hold, and then sped off again. When Matthew finally thought to look up, he saw the other interns all standing on the shore, pointing to him, waving, cheering. They all had removed their gear; the swim period had ended...how long ago?

Matthew was used to being the last one to finish, but this time it wasn't because his hip made him slower. Only as he climbed from the water to the applause of all the other interns did Matthew realize that his hip still ached—probably as much as it did when he had entered the water. But he had forgotten it, forgotten everything.

"Fabulous, Matthew!" Consuelo said, patting him on the back as though he had raced the last leg of their side's relay. "You've made a real friend in Queenie. That's extraordinary."

"But I didn't do anything—," Matthew started to say, but Queenie, behind him still, in the water, answered with a squawking of high-pitched notes.

"We should have videotaped it—you should have seen yourself, Matthew—"

"I'm swimming with Queenie tomorrow!"

"You were flying!"

"Don't kid yourself," Consuelo said. "You did plenty. Queenie's no fool."

On the way to lunch, and all through the meal, the other interns surrounded Matthew with questions. "How did you get Queenie to tow you?"

"Well, I didn't, exactly—," he tried to explain.

"How did she tell you to dive?"

"I guess I just felt—," he said, but then another question interrupted.

"What did it feel like?"

"It all happened so fast," Matthew said, but he did try to describe each thing as he remembered it. If only Matthew could have stopped the time so that he could feel each moment more carefully, individually. If only he could play the whole experience again in slow motion, over and over, until it became more than a regular remembering—a permanent, powerful one that could displace all his days of feeling heavy and clumsy and achy and human. But already the swim had passed, sinking to the bottom to become memory and history.

After the eleven teenagers had seemingly run out of questions about his swim, Lee asked about his hip. Consuelo must have told them all while they watched his ride with Queenie. For the first time in his life, people were interested in his hip—not for all the things it prevented Matthew from doing, but for one thing it had done: It had brought him next to a dolphin.

"When I was eight I had two operations to partly replace the joint," Matthew explained. "It's osteomyelitis, a bone disease. When I'm seventeen or eighteen, they'll do a final replacement. And I'll be fine, they're pretty sure. Perfectly normal. It's just until then—"

"So you can feel the plastic—does it feel any different to you?" Stephen asked.

"You've got a great kick—it doesn't bother your hip?" Lydia asked.

More questions followed that night, and the next day. For each of the following days of dolphin camp, Matthew remained the center of the interns' interest and the center of both dolphin groups. Every other swim Matthew spent with Queenie, stroking her, diving with her, riding beside her, trying to find ways to show Queenie how much he trusted and appreciated her. They dove longer, spun and circled, leaped into the air, somersaulted underwater—they did nearly everything that Matthew had ever imagined in his laps at the swimming pool and nearly everything that Matthew couldn't possibly have imagined.

And the same thing happened in the other group: The dolphins there discovered Matthew's exceptional hip, and during his second swim with them, Tulip offered him a dorsal-fin tow.

Only one of the female interns received dorsal-fin tow before the camp ended, and Stephen had a very short dive with Daisy that ended with him swallowing a lot of water.

Most of the interns had been invited, by one dolphin or another, to touch. But everyone, no matter what they did or didn't do with the dolphins, loved simply sharing the dolphins' own environment and observing, firsthand, these creatures' graceful, comic, thrilling, curious, still unexplainable behavior.

"Isn't there some way to repay Queenie?" Matthew asked Consuelo the day before the camp session ended. "If I could only show her or tell her what she's meant to me! I mean, this has been the greatest thing. Ever. In my life."

"Here," Consuelo said, opening her arms wide. "I'll accept a hug on Queenie's behalf." Matthew gladly joined the embrace. "Actually, Matthew, if she could detect a little plastic, don't you think she could tell more than just that your heart beats? I bet she has a pretty good idea of what's inside that heart. Let's give her credit."

In fourteen days Matthew had learned to use an underwater camera and had taken pictures of each of the dolphins from just inches away. He could recognize each member of both pods. He had crammed two notebooks full with his own observations, four experts' lectures on dolphins and saltwater ecology, and details about the marine habitats of dozens of birds, mollusks, shellfish, flowers, plants, and trees. He had traded addresses with the other interns—two were starting college in September—who had all promised to keep in touch. He had used his crutches whenever he needed them.

But besides all these written and remembered things, and besides the already forgotten sensations that Matthew had to leave in the water with Queenie, Tulip, and the other dolphins, Matthew was heading to the airport with a video of himself swimming with the dolphins. *I wonder if dolphins ever miss anyone—a person, I mean,* Matthew thought, *someone that they've known for a little while.* But there was no one in the taxi he could ask, no one, anywhere, perhaps, who knew the answer as yet.

It would still be several years before Matthew's body would stop growing, his hip would be replaced, and, as his doctors and parents assured him, he would be a person with a perfectly normal hip who didn't need to be exceptionally brave or exceptionally determined or exceptionally patient. It would be another year before Matthew could return to the dolphin research camp, and four more years after that before he would graduate from high school and move to Portland to live near his father aboard a ship of dolphin specialists from an oceanographic institute. But flying above the state of Florida, Matthew, a twelve-year-old soon-to-be seventh grader with osteomyelitis, wouldn't have traded his partly plastic hip for a whole and perfect one of bone. In fact, he wouldn't have traded places—not for a single moment—with anyone who didn't possess a blowhole or the secrets of sonar or the gigantic trust of a dolphin.

Juggling

UNTIL MOTHER ACQUIRED TRINKET, we'd never had a living thing in the house. Just Mother and me—and before I can remember, before he died when I was three, my father. We'd never even had a spider plant. After Mother was in the hospital for kidney stones (which looked just like the aquarium gravel in Mrs. Sams's gourami tank), she brought home the boxes of mints and the cards, but the crowded planters—those she gave to the nurses. Until Trinket, Mother's pet peeves *were* pets: cats, dogs, birds, and the other creatures. Mother was half-right about us not getting a pet, since she's got more than a full-time job, and she's half the household. Usually the reason she gave was the mess pets make, the never-ending cleaning up after them. (But Mom herself isn't all that neat: Her car isn't, the garage isn't, and I'd say the basement is truly trashed.)

The simplest reason for Trinket is that since I've been at boarding school, the house has felt even emptier than Mother can stand. See, Mother decided she had to devote herself to both her job and to night school so she can get the promotion she needs to make us enough money so she doesn't have to worry about school *and* money *and* me. Trinket was her beautician's dog, a Maltese—already house-trained. *Sheila is building a second shop, about an hour out of town, and she just can't keep three dogs,* Mother wrote me (this was a couple weeks ago—almost the only letter she's had time to write, but it doesn't matter, since I call home every week), *and seeing how I obviously loved the dog (I didn't even look twice at the dog!), Sheila tucks this powder-puff of a pooch into my purse after my tinting Friday and tells me, "No woman should live all by her lonesome. Period."* Of course, Mother insists she didn't love or even want Sheila's dog (at the time), she simply thought it was adorable the way she slept in Sheila's open empty drawer. (I *think* Trinket's a she. When I go home next month for summer vacation, I'll see the dog for the first time.) Actually I think Mother did want the dog, even though I now think I know the real reason she says she didn't: Mother's afraid of living things. Not because of something they might do, like chewing or digging up stuff while they're alive, but because of the something they all do at the end, the dying part. Even if you care hard for them, they can still slip away, like my father did. And dogs have shorter lives than husbands and fathers are supposed to have.

I first met Mrs. Edna Sams, who my mother calls Ednut and I call Sam (all her friends call her that, though her husband called *her* Eddie and all his friends called *him* Sam), because she had a parakeet in the middle of her living room picture window. Every morning while I waited for the bus, she would draw the drapes and lift a striped beach towel off the birdcage, as if she were revealing a great surprise. That was a while ago, when I didn't know it was rude to stand in front of a window watching a parakeet. (Sam didn't know it, either; but my mother did. Then Sam invited me inside, so Mother couldn't say I was rude.)

Her pure yellow parakeet is named Mumsy—it either never has sung or, maybe, can't. But it will land on Sam's shoulder when she makes a kissing sound. Sam usually keeps the cage door open; most of the day the bird perches near Sam, watching her sew or read, and at night Mumsy sleeps standing in the cage.

I got in the habit of doing homework at Sam's until Mother came home around six. Or seven. Sam and I would talk about school some, but since that's what Mother and I would talk about, we mostly talked about her husband, who died the same year my father did—which isn't that strange, I guess—and about her children who live in Orlando, and about her grandchildren. One even lives in Australia. But most of our talk was about raising African violets.

At last count—this was spring break, when I was home and everything was fine—Sam had 420 violets, not counting rooting leaves or tiny plants that hadn't bloomed yet. While we talked she scraped suckers (those little extra leaves that form between the leaf stalk and the main stem) and refilled the water in the plant cups. All the windows in her house have three shelves, like extra sills, lined with violets. You can hardly see out, except from Mumsy's window. What you see instead is a landscape of pink and purple and white and blue flowers, and then, mostly hidden in the background, our plain old neighborhood of people and cars moving through the rain or slush.

But Sam's basement is her real greenhouse. She has special fluorescent lights that hang, one after the other, across the entire room. She's filled aquariums with dollhouse-size plants, and plastic shoe boxes with vermiculite and rooting leaves. And it's table after table of violets (some plants are almost two feet across!) in every shade but the impossible ones: yellow, orange, and truly black. But with all that blooming, there isn't a flower smell, like, I don't know, Hawaii is supposed to have.

Sam often sells her plants to nearby florists or to people who just stop by while we're working. Somewhere along the way, I started helping Sam. I guess I just did what she was doing while we were talking. I even learned most of the crazy plant names—hundreds of them: Bright Eyes, Motion in the Ocean, Mrs. Templeton, Shooting Stars. Sam has invented a few hybrids of her own: Pinkanese (a miniature plant that, I guess, reminds her of that dog's frilly face) and Cat's Pajamas (deep blue flowers with white tips). Plants that she has created have won awards. She's not a mad scientist or anything, but she's not just cared for plants, she's created new forms of life.

African violets take more care than I ever figured—but then, all I'd ever seen before Sam's were those spindly, sickly looking, boring violets at the grocery store. Hers are like another species—like some wild bright blooms that are really from an African jungle. Each of Sam's plants is suspended from the rim of a glass that holds water and plant food; and there's a wick, which is just a string that hangs down from the soil, that sucks up the right amount of liquid. Wine goblets, coffee mugs, jelly jars, vases—every container in her house has an African violet growing from it. I even got Mother to start saving jars. And cereal and cracker boxes and Styrofoam packages, which Sam uses to pack up plants for transporting.

"When I remember, I'll save them, but it's just one more thing to juggle," Mother said.

"You don't have to juggle them, Mom," I told her, "just don't trash them."

Mother's a career counselor, but she always calls herself a juggler.

Mother didn't disapprove of my spending time at Sam's, but she did think it was a waste of money to have the sitter waiting at home from three to five (or six or seven) if I was always going to be across the street. She couldn't bring herself to hire Ednut to be my official sitter, but she couldn't *not* have someone at home, either—someone to start dinner and straighten up a little. Sam tried to persuade my mother. "You can pay me for the couple hours I'm with Jonathan, and I can pay him for the couple hours he's working with me, and we can trade dollar bills. He's simply indispensable. I have more plants than minutes in the day." I think that's the first time anyone said the word *indispensable* meaning me.

So much for what Mother called our "discussion," which was really an argument, since I got sent to my room for being a smart-mouth. (I think I said something like, *If you're so busy, then don't worry about me and save yourself some time.* I was sorry afterwards.) Anyway, Mother was willing to save boxes and jars, and she was proud that I could be so helpful when I put my mind to it, but Patty Geiger *was going to stay* at the house. "She's there for emergencies and to take messages with phone numbers that are legible (thank you very much, Jonathan), and to start dinner—and besides those reasons, there's an even better one: Your mother doesn't need a reason." If you want to figure out why...why *anything*— forget reasons.

One day Sam was getting ready for a vacation with her kids in Orlando. She was making turkey chili to take them, and we were wrapping up two enormous violets to take along. Our protective package of boxes and paper-plate collars looked like a birdcage big enough for a dodo or a vulture, but with solid walls. Mumsy even perched on the top.

The chili was cooling—a gigantic pot, full to the brim. It was after six o'clock, so I said good-bye, and since Sam was wearing two oven mitts to move the chili, she blew me a kiss. "In one arm, I'll have ten pounds of frozen chili," Sam said, "and in the other, our violet contraption, and behind me, a skycap with my too-many suitcases." We were both laughing until I reached the door and heard Sam scream, "Mumsy! Jonathan!"

I ran back into the kitchen. Sam was reaching right into the chili pot with her oven mitts. "Turn on the faucet!" she shouted. "Cold water, cold!" She held her mitts under the stream to wash away the chili liquid, revealing a yellow lump in this muddle of brown, like a piece of butter that hadn't melted. "Mumsy! How could she? She perched . . . in the pot!"

Mumsy was alive but in shock, according to the vet. Mother drove the three of us to the clinic—I saw her pull into the driveway from Sam's kitchen window; I didn't even let her turn off the motor. Even though the vet said the bird would be fine, since she'd landed feet-first and only scalded the skin there, Sam thought about canceling her trip.

"She needs ointment on her feet twice a day, and she can't even stand." Mumsy rested on her side at the bottom of the cage, as if the wind had blown her over. Her pink legs stuck straight out and her toes slowly opened and closed. They creaked. "See, a bird can't move its eyes all around like a person or a dog can," Sam explained. "Mumsy has to turn her whole head to see in different directions, and now—now how can I just leave? I'm glad, Jonathan, you're not someone who'd say something like, *For goodness' sake, it's only a bird!* Because when it comes down to it, I'm only an old lady . . . and you're only a young man, and caring is caring because there's no *why* about it. You either care or you don't. And if you do, whatever creature comes into your life becomes a part of that caring, right?"

"Yes, of course," I said, because I understood her point; but I did convince Sam that I could come in and apply the ointment. I could even feed the gouramis (which I had named Goofus and Gallant, after that cartoon in the magazine my great-aunt from Oregon still sends me, like she thinks I'm stuck in first grade. Maybe she bought me a lifetime subscription). And I could look after the violets. *Indispensable.* The whole trip back from the vet's, I knew what Mother had been thinking, even if she hadn't said it: "You see, Jonathan Allen, you see what comes from having little creatures in the house? You think I want that kind of responsibility?" I guess I'm more responsibility than I think I am.

But honestly, that week was easy. The violets, the fish, the tipped-over bird—they all accepted me as their baby-sitter—or house-sitter, I guess. There's really no right word for just caring about animals and plants in a part-time kind of way. It has nothing to do with "sitting," that's for sure. Or what's the right word for the part-time hanging out with someone who isn't a baby? Patty Geiger's not "baby-sitting" me when she studies her college books in our dining room.

Just after that week, I told my mother I thought I might become a biologist one day, and after I announced that, my mother told me, well, fine, that was another good reason she was going to send me to a boarding school in Massachusetts: "The middle schools around here don't even offer zoology and botany." The other good reasons she didn't have to tell me; they probably had a lot to do with Mother's own life, which has been a lot harder than just switching schools.

One time, when I came down for breakfast and she was still writing out some final exam that she'd started when I'd gone to bed, she asked me, "Jonathan, how about if I get you a full-time mother who isn't an overworked career counselor, part-time graduate student, servant to one smart-mouth kid, the most eligible lousy date in town, and a poor sleeper on top of all that?"

"Nah," I answered, because kids sometimes figure out the right answer. "Nah, you're more than enough."

Later we did have a real discussion about school—the kind where both people listen. And then I started Academy boarding school last August. Sam gave me a farewell gift of six violets grown from cuttings I'd helped start. Since then she's sent postcards of violets—I have them lined up below my six real violets in the window; they make two extra sills.

I didn't mind my first semester. I did OK. (OK, I did

better than OK.) I learned to play racquetball—our school has eight indoor courts—and I came out third in our play-offs. I like my roommate, Chip Atherton, who actually doesn't get along with anyone else but me, and Academy keeps us so busy that no one has a chance to think about the real world we're missing or being homesick.

"How come your father sends you dumb postcards instead of an envelope with cash?" Chip asked me when the first violet card arrived signed, *Love, Sam.*

"It's my neighbor—this lady—not my father," I replied, trying to leave it at that.

But every time a card came from Sam, Chip said something like, "Who's sending you flowers, Johnny-boy?" or "Are you going to be a florist someday, Jon-a-than?"

"I'm taking botany, you idiot," I answered him. "You know, plant science? Horticulture. Ever hear of that on your dim planet?" But because I do like Chip more than a lot of the other boys (he tells me all this personal stuff that he doesn't tell anyone else), I try to tell him some of the really interesting things about Sam...like how she's hybridized plants or...well, forget it. There's no explaining one person to another. There's no explaining anything to anyone except maybe what you missed in Latin class yesterday or how to stretch a blade of grass between your thumbs to make a whistle.

This is the first thing Mother said when she picked me up for Christmas vacation: "What in the world are you doing to your record player?" (Not even "Hello," although I knew she meant "Hello," first, and even "I love you," second. You sometimes know what people mean even when they don't say it—love, I mean. It's still kind of better when they do say it.)

"It's not mine, it's an old one the school lent me for my botany project." I'd forgotten how peculiar my dresser looked: " 'The Influence of Rotation on *Helianthus annuus.*' " I was spinning sunflower seeds on the record player at 16 RPMs, which is a whole lot more rotation than the earth's spin. "Four of my potted seeds spin eight hours a day, and four of them spin twelve hours, and four of them are the controls and don't get spun at all." (I had wanted to test the effect of 33 and 45 and 78 RPMs, but Mr. Cheltenham said not to bother, the differences would be slight and the turntable might have a chance of playing a record again after I was done.)

I grabbed my suitcase, slid the seedlings into an orange crate with my violets—they were doing beautifully (that was the first thing Sam said when I walked into her house)—and we headed to the car.

I was just in time to help Sam pack for a two-week visit to Australia; her grandson and his wife had just had a baby. While we refilled all the violet jars and self-watering troughs, we talked about all the same things we had written to one another. Somehow, nothing seems to happen until you're there in person to see the changes or hear the news right where it happened.

So we figured we could finish catching up during my last two weeks of break, and that for the first two, I would be the temporary *caretaker* (that's what Sam decided to call me, which beats *violet/bird/fish-sitter*). The rest of the time I would study or hang out with friends from my old school. Academy was all reports, papers, and projects, and two were due January 11—one being the report on my rotation study. Most of vacation I had our dining room table covered with a newspaper tablecloth, and all the seedlings I'd carefully uprooted were spread in front of each chair: It looked like I'd invited some strange family for dinner. (It didn't really matter, since we hadn't used the dining room since Mother went back to school.)

One day Mother waltzed in with the portable phone covered by her hand. "Mr. Professor?...Ednut calling."

"Hello? Hello, Jonathan? How are you, dear?"

I could immediately tell something was wrong, just the way Mother says she can tell when I'm not telling her something. And two weeks hadn't passed yet—had she come back early? I said I'd run right over, but then Sam replied, "Well, it'll be a long run. I'm in Melbourne. This is long, well, this is longest-distance."

"Wow, I've never talked to Australia before...or... anywhere out of the country. When are you coming home? Isn't this expensive?"

"The operator will worry about cost," she said. "Now, I'm fine, but I'm not coming home right away. I had an accident here, you see. Technically, I had an accident even before I got here—getting off the plane."

I was so shocked I couldn't think of a single thing to say or to ask—there was nothing I could *do*—so I just listened to her expensive sentences.

"It was raining cats and dogs—I feel so silly—the flight

crew people were trying to be helpful, but the landing stairs were so slippery and, four steps from the bottom, your friend here landed on her hip."

I stared at the clock on our stove; even though the second hand moves, it keeps the same time all day: 4:58. I pictured Sam fallen over on her side like Mumsy. "When will you be home?"

"As I said, I am all right, really, but I can't get around too well—"

"Are you in the hospital?"

"Please don't be worried. But it's going to be a cast for a couple of weeks, and this doctor insists: no traveling. Just rest. So you and I have to talk business."

I knew what was coming next. "Look, I'm going to keep taking care of your house. I'll pinch off the dead flowers and mix the feeding solution and mist the cuttings. I can check for mealybugs and mildew—didn't you show me almost everything that's got to be done? For Mumsy and the fish, too."

Sam listened, told me quickly about the seven-and-a-half-pound baby girl, Elsbeth, but then tried to bring up how much she wanted to pay me per day for helping. So I told her about my rotation experiment, and how the longer you rotate a seedling, the more its main root spirals in that direction.

"I've never heard of such a thing," she said. "It almost makes sense, though, when you think about this crazy, dizzying world. Look what it's done to people...our roots are all tangled and spun around. Look at me: born in Russia, living in Ohio, and now I'm here in Australia with my grandson and his family. Now those are twisted-up family roots."

When we hung up, after about ten minutes, I guess, the stove clock still read 4:58, as though Sam had never called and she were just across the street, before the accident. Or maybe, if the clock really was keeping time—keeping it from ever going forward—it had stopped when I was six years old and still reading about Goofus and Gallant, or maybe it had stopped when my father was still alive and the stove was a place where Mother cooked things.

"What could she want all the way from Australia?" Mother called from the pantry. So I explained about her accident. "And when does she think she'll be home? A broken hip can be a major setback for an elderly person. Months."

"Months? It won't take months. She'll be home before I go back to school. Sam isn't that old, Mom."

"Eighty? Eighty isn't that young. She's old enough to be *my* grandmother, sweetheart. Well, I'm a little worried," Mother said. "We could send her flowers—from you and me? Those florists can send them anywhere in the world...Do you want to?" See, Mother likes Sam, it's just that she hasn't had any time to get to know her.

But Sam didn't return to America before I had to leave for school. Two days before we drove back to Academy, a letter arrived from Melbourne.

I didn't remember Sam's handwriting was so jagged. Even the rounded letters were made of broken straight lines. I read it several times and then forced it down the disposal with a lot of water and grinding. What it said was (I memorized it, not really trying to):

Please take Mumsy back to school if you can keep pets, and take Goofus and Gallant, too, but empty most of the tank so that the water doesn't slosh out the whole ride there.

She also said this, which I can't believe:

> *Now, Jon, don't bother anymore with the violets because*
> *I don't need the money from selling them and they were*
> *just a pastime that I've always loved, but now, I think,*
> *it's past time I got rid of them. They're a constant*
> *responsibility—even when I'm at home. So please accept*
> *this check for being such a caring caretaker, looking in*
> *on everything all month.*

And last of all, she said she'd call when she did arrive home, but now the doctors weren't promising her less than two months.

I have her check here in my dresser at school. Did I wonder for one minute what Mother would have said if I asked her if I could stay out of school to take care of a houseful of violets? I didn't need to. Mother was great. She called my Aunt Hat and arranged for her to keep Mumsy until June. She agreed to forward Sam's mail. And then she said we should have a "discussion" (which might have been an argument, except, I guess, Mom let me win) about the violets. I knew Sam couldn't really want them all to die. All 420 plants? Years of work? Wouldn't she want something to do while she was recovering? Her letter wasn't reasonable.

Our first discussion was at dinner, at a restaurant where Mother used to work—she had also been a waitress when she didn't have many clients yet as a career counselor. Mother said, "Jon, you ought to consider the idea that Sam might not be fit to come back—it could be even longer than two months. She's a fragile, elderly woman. How are you going to be the long-distance singlehanded plant-and-animal-sitting caretaker forever? From school?"

"I could do it when I'm back in May, and maybe you could do it, Mom, just for a couple months, or until Sam is back. It's not forever."

"No, it's not forever, but it happens to be four, not a 'couple,' months when I couldn't be busier. I don't know a thing about plants or birds or fish or—I guess I do know what *you* need—but, Jonathan Allen, like it or not, a person has to choose what to care about. And I've made some hard choices, and you, you'll have to as well. Is it going to be your family or your studies? Is it people or animals—or maybe plants?"

I just didn't understand Mother's logic. I thought we were

talking about Sam's fish and Sam's African violets. "Why do I have to choose? It's not that much time. It's not that hard. The gouramis will take you two minutes total, including the walk over and back. And the plants, well, maybe once a week. An hour—"

"It isn't just time, Jonathan," Mother said. "It's—well, there's only so much feeling and responsibility a person can manage. There are only so many hours in the day—if you could stop the clock and spend all the time in the world caring for each and every thing that asks something from you, then it would be different. But still, the heart is only so big—"

"But, Mom, what if... what if 'so big' is big enough? How do you know that your heart isn't big enough? Can't you make it bigger? Is it going to break or something if you love too many things?"

I said that way too loud for a restaurant where everyone knows us. But then, after glaring at me for shouting, Mother said, "Mine did," and then she just gave in and said, "All right—right now, let's drive over to Ednut's. You show me where and how much, and I'll dump in the water. That's all I have to do, huh?"

We worked until ten-thirty, moving all the upstairs plants

into Sam's back bedroom, where there are three windows, and I improvised a plant trough to set the plants inside— just like the basement arrangement. Sure, the plants will stop flowering, and since Mother doesn't know how to fuss with them, they'll probably develop problems, but at least Sam will have her plants. I'm also sure that in three more months, Sam could have them flowering again.

Last week I got a postcard from Sam of an Australian kangaroo paw plant:

The doctor says, slowly but surely, I'm healing. If only I were a violet, I would have already regrown a dozen leaves! I'll hardly need the walker in a month. The stiffness from the cast takes longer than the bones do to heal.

Me, I've written once a week. I haven't said anything about the violets; I did mention that Aunt Hat is keeping Mumsy. It's not that I don't trust Mother, but I really don't know if she's been over to Sam's like she says. She says a lot of the plants are still blooming. She says she even sold four plants to someone who happened to knock one day while she and Trinket were watering. But that could be her way of making me do well in school. All 420—or 416—violets could be dead by now, just the way Sam figures they are, and I won't know for sure until Sam comes home, or until Mother—with Trinket, I guess—drives me home at the end of next month.

Now, in today's mail, there's this letter from Mother saying that one of the gouramis has died:

I promise, Trinket and I have been feeding them right on schedule. (Trinket likes to lick Ednut's kitchen floor.) The other fish is fine, I'm sure, but the water is a little cloudier than before. But there are all those snails on the glass! Isn't it their responsibility to keep the water clear? You didn't teach me how to clean the tank, Jonathan. In case you're wondering, it was the larger fish that died. I'm sorry. (When you get home, we can buy her another one, and maybe she doesn't even have to know that it's a replacement.)

That would be Gallant who died. Actually, I don't know how to clean an aquarium, either. Sam hasn't taught me that yet. Besides dropping a pinch of food in the tank, all I know how to do is lift the lid and hold one fingertip on the surface so that the gouramis come up and make little puckered kisses on my skin—that's not exactly being an expert.

I've been thinking that maybe, instead of just missing your mom or dad, *homesick* could mean a kind of real sickness you get from being away from home. A real disease with symptoms like a headache or a fever or dizziness—because if dizziness can be one of the symptoms (like your roots are being spun around on a record player), then maybe I've been homesick more than I realize. Or, I don't know, maybe it's just what my heart is supposed to feel since I've been thinking about Mumsy and Sam and the violets—and a lot about Mother. I do worry about her more than I think she worries about me, which is the way it should be, because, really, I'm fine. I'm just going to Academy, while she's the one working doubly hard to make enough money so that I can be here, and so that, next year, or the year after, I can be home with her again, when she'll have her master's degree and the promotion she wants, and more time to be my mom. It's complicated.

And I do have to think about school. I got an "Excellent" (we don't get letter grades) on that rotation experiment. In a month I'll be home to a house with a lot more living things than ever before: Mother and Trinket, and maybe Mumsy and Goofus and another fish. And maybe Sam will be there, too, and maybe I'll have to do some caretaking for her. I don't really have anything but baseball practice and my summer reading list for June, July, and August. I won't have to choose between caring about this or that, like Mother said. I'll be able to be indispensable again. I'll show her. It'll be a kind of experiment that I can prove, where I'll just try hard to make my so big heart grow big enough. Hey, Mother's already did: Besides me, she loves Trinket now. And I bet she loves—OK, *likes*—violets, and that's a start.

Mastering the Art

IN WEST VIRGINIA, where there is no ocean, a huge conch shell rested on Dillon's nightstand. His Grandma Pauline sent it from Florida, where she had just moved. (Her back was certain to feel better in a warmer climate.) Sometimes, before bed, Dillon would hold the shell, which was shaped like a giant's ear, to his own ear, and listen to the ocean where his grandmother lived. "It's like a natural telephone," he told his father one evening before bed. "If I were little, I could pretend I'm calling long-distance all the way to the waves of Grandma's beach."

"You can call her on the real phone anytime you like,"

his father replied. He was a practical man, a reporter, who happened to spend a good deal of his day on the telephone.

Dillon did speak with his grandmother every Sunday when his family called, but he still missed her. He missed their field trips—that's what he and his grandmother called their nature hikes, which they always took on the weekends, when Dillon's house would be filled with the clamor of some televised ball game. Dillon's father worked full-time for the *Star-Journal*, covering the major sports leagues. And in his spare time he watched more ball games, either from the couch or from some stadium seat. Dillon did like to go with his father, sit in the press box, and watch his favorite teams in action, but his own spare time was occupied with many other interests—too many, according to his mother, who had to carpool him to every one.

What really drove Dillon crazy was how his parents liked to watch several games at once, with the upstairs portable set stacked on top of the large-screen set in the den, a portable radio tuned to a third game—and sometimes his father would even run out to the garage to hear the score of yet another game that only the car radio could pick up. Usually his parents' friends joined in the TV room's audience, bellowing the idiot coaches' names and cussing out (accidentally) the fumbling players. If Dillon was home during those loud afternoons—if it was raining, say, and he couldn't bike to a friend's house—he would read in his room, impossible though it was to concentrate on anything but their shouts, which all seemed to be addressing him, as though somehow *he'd* let them down. He tried to control his attention, to focus it on his homework or the book he was studying, just the way Master Cho insisted all his students must learn to concentrate; but it didn't work—not until the one day he tried holding that giant conch to his ear and focused on the ocean's roar until it drowned out the voices down the hall.

The one sport that Dillon honestly loved, tae kwon do, which he practiced three times a week in the martial arts room/cafeteria at the community center, didn't really interest his father. The *Star-Journal*'s cub reporter, Nancy Pettingill, sometimes covered less popular sports like martial arts. (A photograph of Dillon's winning team had appeared in the other paper, a suburban weekly, one time, a long time ago.) His mother drove him to tae kwon do lessons and tournaments, but she just read thick novels during his sessions. Dillon didn't really expect her to follow the forms that Master

Cho led the class through: The katas, even though they were all based on fighting movements, weren't quite as exciting as some ninja warrior bloody-combat movie. His sparring routines were more like skating or gymnastics, combined with meditation. Most days the only opponents that Dillon fought, even when he demonstrated the series of balanced kicks, blocks, punches, and strikes for a multiple-assailant attack, were all imaginary; he didn't expect his mother to see them.

But she faithfully attended every class and tournament, sometimes with Dillon's father, who appreciated the discipline even less; and one time they'd even borrowed a friend's camcorder. Many of the parents videotaped their children, probably because they weren't allowed to cheer. They had to show the same respect as all the trainees; during events, only whispering was permitted. So the bleachers weren't filled with parents yelling "Come on, get tough!" or "Don't dribble through the middle," or "Take your time, make it count!" Nobody's parents stared out with scowling, disappointed faces when some boy accidentally missed a pass and cost the team some crucial points. And Dillon's father couldn't offer his usual coaching suggestions to Master Cho, either.

What Dillon liked most about tae kwon do was that he

could see himself improving, which was not true with some of the other sports he played. They were so seasonal—Dillon never got to master his basketball skills before it was time to switch to soccer or football—but Dillon had taken five years of martial arts.

"I know you guys can't see it since I'm really competing with myself," Dillon explained to his parents, "but I'm winning, almost all the time." Even at tournaments, where Dillon often won trophies and ribbons (which made his parents more proud than seeing him pretend to pummel the closet door with knife-hand strikes or topple the La-Z-Boy recliner with roundhouse kicks), his parents couldn't see why he had been better than some other competitor. He'd tried explaining many times: "Well, look at the balance and speed that go into making each movement powerful." But so much of it was interior strength and mental focus that his parents gave up trying. "We're just glad it makes you happy," they'd say. And he gave up explaining, "Well, if you tried looking harder, you might...," since that sounded angry, which was contrary to tae kwon do philosophy: "Respect the Elder and love the Younger."

This last summer his grandmother's back had made her

do more resting than hiking. And since her move, Dillon had found that he missed her apartment, where she'd collected specimens for forty years. It was as crowded as the wildflower fields or creek bottoms they'd explored together. Rather than feel at home in her rooms, Dillon felt a constant almost nervous amazement, which he never felt anywhere else except at, maybe, the NASA Lewis Space Center, which they'd all visited on a vacation once. He missed paging through her fossil and bird-watching field guides, and peering into the towers of glass drawers mounted with her Lepidoptera and Diptera and Hymenoptera collections. ("You know, butterflies, flies, and bees," Dillon translated to his parents, as though he himself hadn't just learned those words from Grandma Pauline.) He missed how his grandmother could point out wildflowers named Dutchman's Breeches, Yellow Goat's-beard, and Skunk Cabbage. He liked how she taught him things (she had retired from teaching high school biology the year Dillon was born) that no one else knew, and no one else in Dillon's life even cared to know—that made the information they shared all the more mysterious and personal, like an art to which he was an apprentice. All the classes and families and genera and species of the plant and animal kingdoms fascinated him. With every word he learned to pronounce and define, Dillon felt—well, those words perfected a little piece of the loud, chaotic, unknown world that was everywhere around him, and closing in, gathering forces... particularly at Lincoln Middle School, which Dillon, along with plenty of kids from the rougher nearby neighborhoods, would be attending this next fall. If he could master the words, just as he was learning to master each movement in tae kwon do, they would help him master his own unfocused powers.

That Latin language of plants and animals was as remote to his parents or to his best friend, Allen, as RBIs, NFL trades, and some of the other sports lingo his father spoke sounded to Dillon and his grandmother. But part of every life is finding those people who speak your language—and that was what Dillon was just discovering.

"When you come in December," Grandma Pauline promised on the telephone, "we'll take our field trips again, but now they'll be beach expeditions! I'm studying the names of Florida's fauna and flora. They're all so different here. Isn't that great, how Florida has *flora* in it? That same root word as for *flower*. By December, I know my back will be perfect."

Every week until winter vacation, Dillon's grandmother mailed him a small package. One week it held a thin, sharp, triangular stick with blunt spines. "It's the tail of a *Limulus*, the North American horseshoe crab—one of the oldest creatures. It's Paleozoic!" his grandmother wrote in the tiny print she used for labeling her slides and specimen boxes. Another week she sent him twenty angel-wing clamshells. Then a sandwich bag of beach glass with edges as soft as pieces of cloud.

"You mean these used to be regular glass, like in our windows?" he asked his mother.

"Or from ketchup bottles or baking dishes or jugs," she replied. "The tides buff and polish them." Dillon's mother had lived in California—she had been a professional surfer—and knew more about beaches than a sand flea. Dillon had only visited the beaches in Virginia a few times—each visit, the tides brought along so many man-o'-war jellyfish that he worried the whole time about being stung and never really enjoyed the ocean.

The next week Grandma Pauline's package contained green beach glass. A red rubber band held a note to one piece: "A present the ocean made especially for you."

"Look! This one has letters on it: FOR D." Dillon rubbed his thumb across the raised letters. "She found beach glass with my initial right on it! FOR D. For *me!*"

Dillon's parents each passed a finger across the letters.

"Her back might be trouble, but she's got the eyes of a hawk," Dillon's father added. "Do they have hawks in Florida, Dillon? What about a pelican's eyes?"

Dillon kept that piece of beach glass in his pants pocket—so smooth, so perfect to rub between his fingers, so thin, like a quarter, it might even have fit into the slot of a phone booth (not that it would have connected him with his grandmother).

Every new package brought winter vacation closer, and also Grandma Pauline (and also the Citrus Bowl, for which his parents had tickets). In fact, Dillon's room began to increasingly resemble his grandmother's new ones—at least, the ones he imagined: something like her West Virginia apartment, but with the addition of a zillion new collections. He imagined sunnier rooms cluttered with beach maps, sketchbooks, botanical charts, drawers of mollusks, baskets of wildflowers waiting to be pressed, and field guides everywhere.

Each time Dillon picked up her sand dollar or her starfish,

one of whose arms had snapped off in the mail, he knew he was holding something his grandmother had discovered. "See this red dot at the end of the starfish arm?" Dillon showed Mrs. Dash, his fifth grade science teacher, and a few kids hanging around before lunch period. "It's called a simple eye. But starfish don't really see so well. They taste and smell the water when they're searching for food." Dillon shared a lot of what his grandmother sent. Somehow, even though Dillon wasn't always interested in the hobbies his friends shared at school, he was genuinely surprised when they didn't have— or at least show—some interest in his.

"In January we're doing a whole ocean unit," Mrs. Dash told him. "Maybe you can save up some things to share— or discover some new things when you're in Florida during break—and we'll use them in our ocean studies."

The Saturday morning that began Dillon's vacation week, he cooked breakfast for his parents. He made his bed, lugged everyone's suitcases to the garage—if only he were old enough, he would have driven his family to the airport at the crack of dawn.

"The plane isn't going anywhere without us," his father

kidded him. "Relax," he said, though his parents were just as excited.

Hours later, when Dillon and his parents finally arrived at his grandmother's apartment, a high-rise that towered thirty-one floors above a stormy ocean, nothing was as Dillon had imagined it. Not even his grandmother. She was, she was—

"You're so tan," Dillon said as he hugged her. The four of them embraced and kissed and started telling stories in the hallway, until Grandma Pauline ordered, "Come in, come in! Why are we standing out here?"

While his parents tackled the luggage again, Dillon shoved open the door to race inside...but he halted abruptly in his tracks, as though he were performing a fake in one of his self-defense routines. This had to be the wrong apartment. These rooms were not Grandma Pauline's; they were almost empty, except for some big furniture. Nothing hung on the walls. Just one bookshelf contained any books at all. Nothing was displayed on the windowsills or counters except for a bowl of oranges and a long parade of holiday cards. Where were all her specimen drawers? The ones from West Virginia?

The ones from her new beach? And, come to think of it, where was the beach? Dillon dashed to the balcony's sliding door, but thunderclouds obscured the view.

"Dillon, my Dillon!" his grandmother called as she joined her grandson rubbing at the foggy glass. "Every day since I've been here, I've tried to imagine you getting a little bigger so I wouldn't be surprised when I saw you, but you've grown even more than I imagined!"

"Grandma, what happened to all your collections?" Dillon asked from within his grandmother's embrace.

"Oh, those. Boxes and boxes and boxes...I hope you won't mind sharing the guest room with them. The movers stacked them there and I haven't touched a one."

"But don't you want all your pictures hung? Aren't you going to display your specimens?"

"I've been so busy getting my tan—"

"Mom, don't be such a kidder," Dillon's father called from the guest room.

"Honestly?" Grandma Pauline replied. "It's that back of mine—my least favorite collection, my old bones! Too much reaching and lifting and bending for right now."

"But now—ta-dah!" Dillon's father said, suspending his

empty suitcase above his head. "The super power-lifters are here. And Dillon's been practicing oriental power-lifting, too, so he's unstoppable—"

"No, I haven't—Dad, you don't lift weights in tae kwon—"

"Whatever," his father said. "I was just kidding. Was *I* that serious when I was a kid, Mom? Dillon, unpack your suitcase so we can go—"

"—for a beach walk!" Dillon supplied, although he knew that really ought to have been a question.

Not after lunch, when Grandma Pauline took them to her apartment's indoor pool for a swim, and not before dinner, when the thunderstorm began to move out to sea, but just before dark, when the sun, as though melting in the ocean, spread an orange slick toward the beach, Dillon and his family at last headed for the water. His parents stacked their shoes on a bench and raced each other into the loud, foaming waves.

Grandma Pauline settled herself on the bench. "I'll sit here and guard shoes," she told Dillon as he finished unknotting his high-tops.

"No, you come, too," Dillon said. "It's still light enough, maybe we'll find some new things tonight."

"No, tonight you just visit the ocean a little. Tomorrow, maybe, we'll talk about field trips," she replied.

Barefoot at last, Dillon reached to pull his grandmother's hand. "No, let's collect stuff now, Grandma, together."

"Sweetest, I don't have the heart to tell you this, but who knew? Your old grandmother here isn't too good at beach hiking. Regular walking, fine, but sinking-in-the-sand walking? Well, it aggravates my back."

"Never? You can't walk on the beach ever?"

Grandma Pauline pulled Dillon's hand to bring him closer. "Maybe in another month or so, my doctor thinks," she answered. "I'm doing my exercises. It's getting stronger. I've moved here, and I'm certainly not going to live in my apartment all day long, so let's say I've met my new challenge. So for now, a little walk to dip my toes, fine. But honest-to-goodness hiking, no, that's out—"

"But what about all those—those whelks you sent me, Grandma? The angel-wings and razor clams and starfish?"

"Come on, Dillon, water's warm!" his father called from the surf.

"In a minute," Dillon shouted back, louder than necessary to reach the water.

"Dillon, darling, I would collect the sun and moon for you if I could, but for now, I can only visit the store filled with these natural wonders where I bought you those things."

"But I thought you picked them!"

"Well, I did pick them, I picked them out for you at the shell store. And my next-door neighbors, Connie and Jane, they gathered some of the beach glass. But for now..."

"So who's going to go on field trips with me now—like Mom and Dad are going to let me wander off myself? And they don't care about collecting anything but—but scores!" Dillon tugged free from his grandmother and ran to the water, which was *not* warm, at least not until his mother snuck up, dunked him from behind, and told him that she wasn't going to spend seven days with someone who was going to pout like a baby the whole time.

Sunday morning the storm weakened, then worsened. While his parents showed Grandma Pauline some scrapbooks they'd brought of Dillon's Halloween party and the newspaper's Thanksgiving benefit for local hunger agencies, Dillon sat on his grandmother's balcony listening to the waves crashing on the empty beach. He practiced a few of his tae kwon do katas, but there wasn't really enough room. He wanted to practice on the beach. Master Cho said that in Korea he had taught on the beach, with trainees performing their meditations right in the surf. Dillon tried to center himself, control his wandering thoughts, concentrate on his movements, but he was listening to the wind instead, as it bent palm trees, tipped over table umbrellas at the pool, and forced seagulls to dip and bounce in flight.

He ended up writing a postcard to Allen back home. His grandmother's apartment building had been printed on one side; Dillon drew a face on one of the twenty-seventh floor's balconies and wrote, *This is me.* On the other side he wrote:

> *I bet it's better weather there in Wheeling. Mom says if it rains all seven days she's going to need a real vacation when we get back. My grandma can't even walk on the beach. I hope I never get a back problem. I don't know if I'll get to collect anything for school. See you after the New Year.*

Sunday afternoon, while his parents attended the Citrus Bowl, Dillon and his grandmother were going to an indoor mall, even though Dillon didn't want to go. "Why did we fly all the way to Florida, just to go inside some stupid mall?" he argued.

"You didn't want to go to the game, which was your decision, so—"

Dillon didn't let his father finish. "So I'm stuck shopping. Great."

"You're going to be stuck with a lot worse than that if you don't change your attitude, mister," his father said, concluding the discussion just as Grandma Pauline knocked on the guest room door.

"OK, time for me to spoil my one and only grandson. Ready?"

Those four hours were their first real time to talk together, not that Dillon had anything particular that he wanted to talk to her about. He didn't want to talk, he wanted to *do* something, which of course could include talking. He wanted to go on a field trip.

"Your folks told me you just advanced another belt in tae

kwon do," his grandmother said. "That's great! So, tell me about it."

"It's my third one." But short of demonstrating one of the katas in the middle of the food court, Dillon didn't figure there was anything else to say about it. "I'm getting better. Master Cho says I'm sort of inconsistent, but when I'm focused, I'm really good."

"I see," his grandmother said, but Dillon didn't expect her to see at all.

"It's sort of like being a runner, I guess," Dillon said. "Unless you're also a runner, running alongside me, you can't really know what's so great about running, because running is so dumb, really, like just running in a circle for an hour."

On the other hand, Dillon couldn't just ask his grandmother to start lecturing on the life cycle of some mollusk or crustacean that neither of them had even seen yet. For the first time, Dillon thought of the sixty years separating him from his grandmother.

"Should we rest awhile, Grandma?" Dillon remembered to ask every so often.

Later they saw a movie about aliens that ended up being

too gory for Grandma Pauline (Dillon thought it wasn't as gory as some he'd seen), and then, for dinner, they met Dillon's parents, who were deliriously excited since their team had won the Citrus Bowl with a last-minute touchdown. All through dinner they kept exclaiming, "What a game!" and waving a stick with a pom-pom at one end that they'd brought back for Dillon. "You both should have been there! We should have got you both tickets—"

"It's like having dinner with cheerleaders," Grandma Pauline whispered as they passed around several dishes from the menu of the Cuban restaurant that she had thought Dillon would especially like. And he tried. But plantains? He'd never tasted plantains before; they were weird, like hot bananas.

Then, because the drizzle continued, they drove to an outdoor bazaar: little booths under canvas tarps selling everything from ugly fruit to cowrie-shell necklaces, from Mexican pottery to wind chimes. Several tents held spectacular arrays of ocean life that Dillon had never seen before, not even in books. Scallop shells larger than a sink. Bins of whole horseshoe crabs. Shark's teeth. Barrels of starfish: ones as little as the gold stars Dillon's piano teacher used to place on his assignments, fat ones and slender spidery ones, and some as large and bristly as a welcome mat.

"They hire deep-sea divers to gather those," Grandma Pauline explained, hoping Dillon wouldn't be disappointed by what her shores might wash up in the next few days. "Pick out a few things for your school project. Your dad told me a little about it. We can research them when we get home."

Dillon wandered among the aisles. Sponges. Spiny urchins. Brain coral. Sand dollars smaller than dimes, larger than plates. Cowries, periwinkles, enormous conchs stuffed with moss and a plant his grandmother called a bromeliad.

Grandma Pauline sifted through the bins, holding up items for Dillon to consider. There was even a section brimming with beach glass. Some pieces had letters on them: VT, R, LY, OR DEPOSIT. "I don't want any of these! I want to find my own shells," Dillon finally announced, stomping out of the booth, "...on the beach!" But it had already grown dark before the storm finally passed—too dark and chilly for any beach walk, even if his parents would have let him go after that disrespectful outburst.

————

Grandma Pauline woke Dillon at six-thirty the following bright morning. She whispered, "Wait too late, and all the tourists will get the best shells. We have to be first!"

"But I thought you couldn't—"

"Shh, don't wake the cheerleaders. No questions. Hurry!"

Dillon pulled on his clothes and joined his grandmother at the door. She held a canvas sack with binoculars, a sketchbook, field guides, and an assortment of plastic bags and buckets. Outside the gate to the beach, a man stood beside a dune buggy. "Right on schedule." Grandma Pauline winked to the man. "Enrique, meet my favorite grandson, Dillon. Dillon, this is my favorite groundskeeper here at the apartment."

"Your grandmother is *my* favorite, too," Enrique said. "She helps with the flowers every day. Climb aboard, *amigo. Mucho gusto.*"

"That means 'Nice to meet you,' " Grandma Pauline said. "I don't know much more Spanish than that. Enrique's teaching me a little."

"*Sí, aprendia muy rápido.*"

"*Mucho gusto,*" Dillon offered in return. "I've had a few months. In school. Of Spanish, I mean." He was too sleepy to pronounce anything, even English, correctly. "Are we re-ally going on a field trip?"

"Well, I had to figure out something, didn't I? And Enrique knows the best shell-collecting beaches around here—"

"In the whole state," Enrique said.

"So I get to ride along while you do the hard part that's not for old ladies."

"Just wait—I'm going to find so many specimens!" Dillon exclaimed, hugging his grandmother. "We should have brought my suitcase to hold them all!"

It didn't take long for Enrique to conduct them to the first of several perfect spots. He drove right into the surf of a white beach cluttered with rounded stones, bits of shells as thick as a gravel driveway, swirls of sand stamped with seagull prints, and bubbling holes where some small creature was digging or breathing. Right alongside the dune buggy, Dillon found dozens of whelks, a piece of driftwood encrusted with volcano-shaped barnacles, and one intact crab skeleton.

Enrique opened the dune buggy's umbrella, and Grandma Pauline sat on the seat back leafing through field guides. She pointed to a matching picture of the crab. "What do you think? Fiddler crab? That's the genus *Uca*. See how one front claw is bigger? Which reminds me, let's put some sunscreen on you before you're as red as a cooked crab. The rays are still strong this early."

Stooped over, picking among the uncountable choices the waves had tossed up that morning, Dillon zigzagged down the beach, talking nonstop to his grandmother. She had placed the fiddler crab at the top of her open sketchbook and begun a drawing. Every so many feet, Dillon would run back to see her progress, or to show Grandma Pauline and Enrique something that he'd found. Sometimes Enrique started the dune buggy and caught up with him.

"What's this one called? It's kind of like one you sent me, Grandma, only, it's—"

"*Mm.*" Grandma Pauline flipped the pages in her guide.

"In Spanish, we call it *caracol*," Enrique said. "And that oyster there, we call *ostra*, and *cangrejos* is our word for crabs."

Dillon and his grandmother pronounced each of the Spanish words again with Enrique. "See, I'm learning, too," Grandma Pauline added. "Florida is teaching me lots of things I didn't even plan on learning."

Just as his parents settled down for breakfast, Dillon bolted into the apartment, hauling his treasures to the table. "We had the luckiest morning," Dillon proclaimed, dumping a sample—an assortment of beach glass—onto the table.

"No, no, not for breakfast. I want a whole glass—with coffee in it! Or a mug!" his father said.

"Look-it! Thirty-seven pieces, in one morning," Dillon announced. One by one, he held up the other things he'd found: blue limpets, slipper limpets, cap-of-liberty shells, moonshells, dogwhelks, oysterdrills, periwinkles, cockles, and helmet shells. One bucket held driftwood smooth as bones, oyster shells as large as Dillon's hand, and a plum-size lead fishing weight.

"So the storm blew over after all," Dillon's mother said. "And I see your grandmother's also overlooked last night's little storming out of the—"

"No apology necessary. That's all behind us," Grandma Pauline said. "No one likes to be disappointed. And I'm living proof of that!"

For part of the afternoon, Dillon and his grandmother washed and dried each specimen, and lined them up along the kitchen counter. "We're going out to eat, anyway!" She laughed. And for the other part, Dillon invited his grand-mother to watch him practice his tae kwon do on the beach. He even tried to teach her a few simple steps (*not* kicks). She followed along—the movements weren't hard to imitate, just hard to perfect. "You know, Grandma, you could probably really help your back taking tae kwon do. You're not too old, really. All the great masters are elders, like you."

"I think I'm done mastering new things, Dillon, but thanks for the compliment."

"No, really, it would help you protect yourself, too, like if—"

"Dillon, dear, I feel perfectly safe. My back is the only opponent I'm worried about. And that's more of an internal fight."

"But that's what tae kwon do is about," Dillon persisted. "The harmony of your inner being and your outer—"

"Dillon, trust me. Inner, outer—never mind. You master this tae kwon do you're so good at, and I'll master . . . oh, I don't know, just being the perfect grandmother."

Each day for the rest of their stay, Dillon's family did something he'd never done before: deep-sea fishing or visiting a parrot jungle or driving through the Everglades. But every day Dillon did manage to practice tae kwon do on the beach. In fact, a sixty-year-old man named Hubert, who had achieved a green belt during the army, saw Dillon from his balcony and joined him for the last two mornings. (No, Hubert didn't think he'd want to become Dillon's grandmother's instructor.)

Each day Dillon also swam with his parents (and without man-o'-wars!) in the ocean, where the waves were so huge his mother kept wishing for a surfboard until one wave stole the goggles right off her face. And then he spent a couple of hours hunting along the beach while his mother and father unpacked box after box from Grandma Pauline's guest room.

Enrique met them again on Thursday morning, and Grandma Pauline drove her own car to a close-by beach on Friday, hiking along the boardwalk while Dillon searched the surf.

By their last expedition, Dillon had forgotten that his grandmother's bad back couldn't endure such a field trip. She seemed to have forgotten, too. If she hadn't been waiting with her field guides on a nearby bench, she and Dillon would have looked up each specimen back at the apartment, after which they would have soaked it and cleaned it with a toothbrush, and set it along a windowsill or bookshelf. Dillon had found incredible things, including the picked-clean jawbone of a moray eel and his own giant conch shell (it wasn't nearly as beautiful as the one on his nightstand at home or as large as the ones they'd seen at the bazaar).

Every flat surface of Grandma Pauline's apartment had been turned into a display. Dillon's parents had entirely cleared the guest room of boxes; it now had room for guests...just as they were leaving. The rest of his grand-mother's rooms were as crowded as they had been in West Virginia.

Early Saturday morning, as her family packed, Grandma Pauline mixed up the batter for her famous picture-pancakes. She could pour a stream of batter into almost any shape that someone named, and that morning her skillet filled with amazing creatures from the ocean.

"Make mine a *cangrejo*, Grandma," Dillon requested.

"A what?" his mother asked. "I don't even know what you two are talking about. Just make mine a silver dollar."

"It's Spanish, Mom. For 'crab,'" Dillon replied. "You know, pincers, a shell—"

"Well, pardon my ignorance, I happen to have taken

French," his mother answered, "though that was back when you'd sit on my lap and talk a little more kindly to your mother."

"Sorry," Dillon said. "Enrique taught Grandma and me all these great words, and I was just practicing."

"It's a shame he didn't teach a little more respect," his mother added.

"Master Cho's teaching me that. But...I'm inconsistent," Dillon said in a softer, embarrassed voice.

"We've all had the best time, Mom," Dillon's father said, serving himself seconds—a huge starfish pancake. "And I bet that if you felt up for it, spring break you could have another visitor. That is, if Dillon felt comfortable flying by himself..."

"Really? Sure! Of course, yes!" he replied. "Grandma, your back will be feeling absolutely perfect then."

"Let's see how things go. Your school marks, as well as your smart remarks," his mother concluded.

"Something to look forward to! I always like that," Grandma Pauline said. "Now you three finish eating, and let me start packing up all of Dillon's stuff."

"I'm already packed, Grandma," Dillon replied.

"No, look around. All your specimens, all your beach glass and shell collections." Grandma Pauline began to gather a row of crab shells from the counter. "And, what do you know, I have boxes galore for packing them all safely for the plane—"

"No, stop! They're yours, Grandma," Dillon almost shouted as he slid his chair back.

"What do you mean *mine*? You gathered them..."

"Dillon, sit tight," his father ordered.

"Grandma, it's your collection, I just picked them for you! You need them for your displays here!" Dillon answered as he reached for his grandmother's hands.

"Darling, no, you take them, I'll—"

"Sweetheart," his mother joined in, "I thought you wanted these for school?"

"I packed the eel jawbone, a few urchins, and a few of the driftwood pieces, but the rest of the things, Grandma's already sent me at home—and she doesn't have any herself."

"Gee, Mom, that sounds fair," Dillon's father added. "Dillon has the ones you got for him and now you have the ones he got for you."

"Right," Dillon said. "Plus, when you start taking your own field trips, you can send me more then."

"All right, then, I give up," Grandma Pauline said. "Fair is fair. So let me trade you some of my sketches. Maybe the fiddler crab picture and some others? You could share those at school, couldn't you, Dillon?"

Grandma Pauline reached around her grandson's chair to hug him. "I thought I was going to miss you all even more now that my empty rooms have been filled with people for a week. But now this place is so full—all my West Virginia collections and all these new Florida specimens—I don't see how I could be missing anything!"

"But we'll still miss you, Mom," Dillon's father replied. "I know Dillon will, right?"

"*Absolutamente*," he replied. "Absolutely, I mean."

"Aren't you going to still call on Sundays?" she asked.

"Sure, now Dillon's conch can ring you up on the conch shell he's found you," Dillon's father joked as he grabbed the large shell on the counter.

"Oh yeah." Dillon laughed. "At home I hold the conch you sent me to my ear and I can hear your ocean waves. It's sort of like a telephone."

Grandma Pauline picked up the conch, which really was no bigger than her ear, and listened carefully. Everyone else at the table sat still, as if they all expected to hear something if they were quiet enough.

"Hmm. No waves inside this one. *Hello, hello, Dillon? Are you there?*" Grandma tapped the conch very seriously. "Oh, of course you're not there, you're right here, so you can't be home to answer me."

"*Abuela, estás loca.*" Dillon laughed.

"You both are," his father said, "whatever you just said."

Pretending to hang up, Grandma Pauline placed the shell back in the row of her new specimens. "I'll try again later. *Collect!*"

The Walkers of Hawthorn Park

WHENEVER FRAYDA THINKS of gardens or flowers or block parties or the word *boyfriend,* whenever she sees a dog or a cat or a person who seems to have no one to look after them, she remembers the summer spent at her grandmother's house. That summer lasted longer than all the other summers, which always start so early, before school is even over, and always end so suddenly, before it should be time again for school. But that Ohio summer lasted—not because it held more days and nights or because it grew warm earlier than usual or cold later than usual—but simply because so many things reminded her of those two gardens where she spent the three months before she entered middle school.

Frayda had only visited Ohio for long weekends before that. Her home had always been Florida, where every month blossomed with one fruit or another and something always needed plucking and tweaking. (That's what her grandmother Nana Clara called any kind of gardening, even if it was only watering or raking.) But from June 3 until the Labor Day block party on Hawthorn Park, Frayda had arranged to live with her mother's mother. Meanwhile her family (that is, her mother, stepfather, and two half-brothers) moved from their condominium into a house they'd been building for over a year. Meanwhile her father and his girlfriend in St. Petersburg spent their summer kissing (or so it seemed likely to Frayda, recalling her recent visits). Meanwhile her best friend, Gracie, was packed off to summer camp in Vermont. Frayda had hoped this summer vacation would be a little less confusing: She could be with one person, her grandmother, instead of having to be constantly introduced to new people in both of her parents' neighborhoods, both of their swimming pools, both of their ever-shifting worlds. Frayda had hoped her summer might be a little closer to normal—although, for the last few years, "normal" really meant all the changes that bullied her family from place to place.

Frayda enjoyed part of every day that summer at the swim club where her grandmother belonged. (*Nana Clara spends her afternoons on the deck playing mah-jongg in her swimsuit, though she never swims,* Frayda wrote Gracie.) She usually had lunch at the snack bar, attended a tennis class, and read lots of books borrowed from the largest, grandest library she'd ever seen. (*You could fit our whole little dinky branch in the lobby of this one!*) But almost every other daylight hour, she worked alongside her grandmother in the enormous gardens that spanned her front, back, and both side yards. (*You wouldn't believe this place. Flowers everywhere! Vegetables everywhere else. I mean it! There's hardly any lawn.*)

Truly, Frayda's grandmother had the greenest thumb in the neighborhood, and she managed to grow vines, fruits, and vegetables that weren't supposed to survive Ohio's fickle weather. She planted the basic fruits and vegetables to be peeled or stewed, preserved or pickled, frozen or canned. She sowed all the table-ready things like radishes (seven kinds) and lettuces. (*She's got enough to feed the rabbits, and most of her human neighbors, too,* Frayda wrote.) While she couldn't grow the persimmons, limes, mandarin oranges, and papayas that flourished on the grounds of Frayda's soon-to-be-old condominium, Nana Clara raised vegetables that Frayda had never seen, let alone tasted. But by Labor Day Frayda had seen, tasted, watered, harvested, and helped cook white eggplants, orange-striped beets, parsnips, apple-shaped cucumbers, cucumber-shaped radishes, polka-dotted shelling beans, arugula, Savoy cabbage, and yellow, orange, and red tomatoes that ranged in size from squat red cushions to tiny yellow pears—and that's just what she could fit in the painting she would make in art class the first day of middle school, the day after she returned to Florida.

Nana Clara lived in a hundred-year-old neighborhood. One of every two houses had either just been painted or was badly in need of a new coat. Most of her neighbors had raised their children in those houses and the vacant bedrooms waited for some grandchild to spend the night. The day Frayda arrived, Nana Clara took her on a walking tour of the block and introduced her to all the families she knew—some she'd known for thirty years—even those that didn't have any children Frayda's age.

Right next door stood one of the largest houses, a group

home where no children lived. "Here, sweetest heart, though they're our closest neighbors, I have to tell you, stay away. Basically, the folks who live here have no family to care for them, and it's care they need. So they share this home—eight or nine adults—and nurses and aides come to look after them. It's a family of sorts, but not a happy one."

"Are they sick?" Frayda asked.

"I'm a neighbor, not a doctor, but I sense that some are better, while some are worse—it's their minds, I think. I feel sorry for them—don't get me started. Just believe me when I tell you, everywhere else on the block...fine, enjoy, visit. But here, here I'll just ask you to avoid."

Nana Clara bent to pick up an empty cigarette packet from the sidewalk. "So tragic. Here, in the middle of our nice-enough neighborhood, are a house and a yard that are even more neglected than the occupants are. Our neighborhood association has tried everything. Over the last ten years, we've written landlords, commissions, health inspectors... we've talked ourselves out." Nana Clara stopped and stared at the group home as though waiting to be reminded of something. "How old were you when your grandfather still had the pharmacy? Oh, probably still in diapers. Anyway, we delivered prescriptions sometimes to places like this one, all over the city—and I remember group homes where the people were goers and doers—always visiting, baking, and shopping together. But here..."

"So what's wrong at this one?" Frayda asked.

"I don't know. I only know symptoms: They leave me paper bags with empty wine bottles in my hedges; I say hello and most of them won't even say hello back; used to be a man there who liked to shout at me—scared me half to death—in my own yard... And see: My sidewalks are covered with the cigarette butts from their walks... I told myself, *Don't get started,* and—too late—I'm already worked up. Promise me you'll just ignore them. If someone talks to you or calls you, I want you to just continue walking."

Frayda listened carefully, although instead of frightening her, Nana Clara's words fascinated Frayda, who loved her grandmother's talking. Her talk about anything. Her voice had a little Yiddish accent mixed in with her Ohio voice, and it was the voice of stories and little-known facts and memories of things Frayda had never known or maybe had forgotten. It almost never spoke of Frayda's "attitude," or Frayda's need to try harder to meet people, or Frayda taking more responsibility, or the other things her parents were always talking about.

"And you want to hear the worst?" Nana Clara continued when they arrived on the top step of her own front porch. "This spring, the same people who own this group home wanted to buy Mrs. Levitan's house, the yellowish brick one over there. Another group home on the same block? Why, if they can't take care of these people and this property, should anyone let them make another one? This is what I told the council members."

"Did everyone agree with you? Did you win?" Frayda asked.

"Win? There's no winning at this, only more waiting until the same problem comes up again, somewhere else in the neighborhood. Look at it: Their so-called landscaping is all stink trees that no one has planted, bushes that block the sidewalk, and their lawn?—it's crabgrass, which, when someone finally gets around to mowing, covers the sidewalks until it blows away. And then there's all their overflowing trash!"

Frayda did know the group home's blue Dumpster, across the alley from Nana's house; just that morning, she and her grandmother had picked up the contents of two trash bags that alley cats had torn open, which had blown into her hedges.

It saddened Frayda to imagine her grandmother living all by herself next door to such ongoing annoyances and disturbances. "Well, at least they've planted all those morning glories along the fence," Frayda pointed out.

"Those, darling," Nana Clara said with a laugh, "those are all volunteers from *my* garden."

Frayda gave her grandmother a puzzled look. "Volunteers?"

"Sure. That's what you call plants that just pop up anywhere...unexpected guests. In my yard I've got volunteer columbines, and little dill plants that spring up all around the garden, and cherry tomatoes galore. All volunteers. Those morning glories of mine were just seeds that blew across the alley and agreed to grow there—no one invited them and no one has cared a hoot for them since."

"What's the difference between a weed and a volunteer?" Frayda asked.

"Oy, such questions. Is that all you do at home? Ask questions? Let me think on it."

———

Despite, or maybe because of, Nana Clara's warning to ignore the residents of the home, Frayda couldn't help but notice their comings and goings throughout the day, each one announced by the loud banging of a screen door that certainly must have awakened anyone resting inside. While Shawna, a girl from next door, taught Frayda some of her drill squad routines (she was trying out for the team) on the front sidewalk, someone from the home always interrupted them circling the block as though it were a lap at some racetrack for walkers. How could Frayda not notice the other people from the home smoking cigarettes and waiting—was it for the race to end, or maybe to begin?—on the brightly painted metal chairs that formed a half-circle on the lawn facing Nana Clara's backyard and Frayda's own second-floor window.

Frayda was glad, in a way, that Nana Clara told her not to speak with the group home residents. Fewer people to meet. Actually, it wasn't shyness but fatigue that kept Frayda from being as outgoing as other people would have her be. Frayda was tired of explaining about her broken-up and put-back-together family. Her father's two remarriages. Her six stepbrothers and -sisters, and her two half-sisters. Frayda had tired of making friends only to give them up a couple months later, when one half of her family decided to move again. She had started three different schools since second grade and relocated to four cities since her parents first divorced. And now Frayda had two sets of friends—one in her real mother's neighborhood and one in her real father's apartment complex an hour away.

And that's why when a woman, maybe the same age as Frayda's grandmother, strolled right into Nana Clara's yard and stripped several daisies from their stalks, Frayda assumed that she must be one of Nana's friends and spoke right up. "If you think those daisies are gigantic, we've got even bigger ones in back!" But then the woman turned, and Frayda recognized her as one of the group home neighbors and knew that Nana Clara probably hadn't invited her over to pick flowers.

"Beautiful. I need them. For my boyfriend," the woman said, telling the flowers instead of Frayda.

You have a "boyfriend"? Frayda thought. *My grandmother would never use that word if she ever decided to find a new husband.* But then, aloud, she said, "Does my grandmother—I mean, is it OK for you to be taking her daisies?"

"Now we'll have flowers for lunch," she replied, as if that

were any kind of answer, and then proceeded through the opening in the privet hedge.

Frayda quickly learned to distinguish the people who shared the group home. One of the residents never looked up as he walked—not even over the hedge into Nana Clara's gardens. He stared at the sidewalk as though it were something important to read, like the headlines that changed every day. Another man wore a winter coat—this was summer!

Shawna told her the names of all the residents. No, not the names, but what the kids on the block called them: "There's Smokestack," Shawna recited. "Guess what he does all day. The guy who always carries the plastic shopping bags is Baggie. Barker is the really tall guy who barks back at the dogs. And Flower Girl is the one who's always stealing flowers from our yards—your grandma's especially. I'm forgetting some. We just call them all the Walkers—like they're one family with that name—since all we ever see them do is walk."

"How come they walk so much?" Frayda wondered.

"Because they aren't allowed to smoke inside," Shawna said.

"Then how come they smoke so much?"

"Because they don't have anything else to do; just smoke and be crazy."

"Walking and smoking would make me crazy," Frayda said.

After dinner, while Frayda plucked and tweaked with Nana (that day it was transplanting beet seedlings), Frayda asked her grandmother again about the corner home. "Shawna says the people there are crazy. Does that mean retarded? I mean, is that an insane asylum next door?"

"What are they? When did you become queen of questions? Well, let's say, whatever their differences, they all need a place to live and they can't live alone," Nana Clara answered. "Maybe, if this were years ago, some might be living in an asylum . . . for all the good that would do." Nana Clara shook her head back and forth and reached to hug Frayda.

"I remember, when I was growing up, there weren't group homes. No, we had our share of crazy people, a few people with more than their fair share of problems. But the neighborhood, all of us there, we looked out a little extra for these persons. Took turns making extra stew. We made sure there were enough blankets in freezing weather. Passed along the old winter coats. But today—I could be wrong—today it seems people are all the time looking out for themselves. No one says they have time anymore for the looking-out for others. And since your grandfather died, being alone and all, I keep to myself a little more."

Frayda tried to think about the neighborhoods she knew in Florida, but she couldn't remember anything like a group home. Finally she asked, "Do the people from the group home go to your block party?"

"Our Labor Day party? Oh, they're certainly invited, but no, no one's ever come that I recall. And I remember pretty much, because no one wants to miss the food. Everyone on the block cooks some specialty—and what cooks we've got! Once a year I get a slice of Mrs. Balduccini's almond cake, and once a year a little of Mr. Forest's pistachio ice cream that I bet you'll help crank. It's food enough to feed an army...even though, this year, it will mean you'll be leaving for home the next day."

"Do you know any of them next door? Personally?" Frayda asked.

"Darling, you have more questions than I have answers. No, I'm sorry—they're not in my mah-jongg club and we don't borrow cups of sugar back and forth. They're harmless people—I don't think one of them would hurt a fly, let alone another person...Well, wait...that one woman certainly hurts my flowers! One day I'll plant a cutting garden just for her, right in my front yard; then, at least, I'll know which flowers she's taking."

"Oh, her—I saw her—" Frayda was about to tell her grandmother about the woman stealing the daisies for her boyfriend when the loud *rrreee* of a gunning motor filled the air. A tall man in a white jersey, a college kid, probably, had started up a rototiller at the alley-edge of the Walkers' lot. The bouncing, churning machine began to chew up the lawn, yanking the man behind it. His arms flapped up and down from the vibration. In the ring of painted metal chairs, five residents smoked cigarettes and watched the new entertainment.

"The middle of June, and they're just now putting in a garden?" Nana Clara said, shrugging her shoulders. "This is a first."

The rumbling, clanking noise of turning-over-and-over earth lasted all evening, even after dark, when Frayda finally drifted off to sleep.

———

In the morning, from the bedroom window that was hers for the summer, Frayda could see that where there had been only crabgrass and creeping mint was now a garden. Rows of seedlings filled half the square, and labeled stakes showed where seeds were being planted in the other half; the same young man (had he been working all night?) was drawing channels into the dirt with his finger and sprinkling in seeds. The person Shawna called Baggie stood behind the gardener, holding a hose. A mist leaked from the nozzle, spraying a rainbow, a giant halo around the gardener, though there was nothing heaven-sent about him.

For the next few weeks, the man who created the garden visited the plot with one or another of the Walkers; he demonstrated how much to water and which were weeds. Frayda could hear his voice across the alley: "Try to step in between the rows...Grab the weeds close to the ground—no, no, like this—we have to get the roots, too."

But by the end of July, the group home's gardener no longer came out of the house. ("He probably went backpacking up some mountain—they never stay long," Nana Clara suggested.) Not one of the Walkers continued the watering or weeding. No one even visited the plot. All the plucking and tweaking that Frayda and her grandmother were doing in their own garden, someone should have been doing in the group home garden. From her summer window, Frayda could see that their lettuce needed thinning and their fallen-over tomato plants had to be staked. "Nana Clara, have you looked at the garden next door?" Frayda asked at breakfast, eating cereal topped with blueberries from Nana Clara's bushes. "They're just letting it all go to weeds."

"Well, who's going to care about the garden when no one cares about the people?" Nana Clara closed the newspaper she'd been skimming. "You know, I think this same question all the time when I see a dog fenced in a tiny run, or barking all day long in a trash-filled yard—and it's pouring down rain, or it's just blazing hot—I think, *Well, what's it like inside that house? What kind of life do the children have who live there?* So if the group home garden is ignored, how is it inside there? Those poor people were left there just like those plants in that half-started garden—"

"But don't you think the people would really like gardening if they knew how?" Frayda asked. "Couldn't you teach them if that other guy is gone?"

"Me? I can't even get a hello out of them, and now I'm

going to give gardening lessons? Maybe I should be ashamed, but that group home has been here ten years and in ten years I've tried my best to improve things there, but friendly? No, I haven't done all that much in the way of friendly—I don't know who on the block has."

Although Frayda honestly didn't have a plan, the next afternoon, while her grandmother took her nap, she walked to the mailbox and couldn't help but notice the bright red radish heads peeking above the ground in the group home garden. Chickweed and kudzu were choking most of the peppers. Maybe if she just picked the radishes and handed them to someone without talking, that wouldn't really be disobeying Nana Clara. But then Frayda decided that she could just *announce* one thing (that isn't the same as "talking"). She wouldn't even have to step into the yard.

"Excuse me, your radishes are ready," Frayda called to the assembly of people in the chair circle.

Someone, Frayda couldn't tell which one, called back, "Hello."

"I think your radishes are ready," she repeated.

One of the Walkers shook his head no very violently, as if he absolutely knew better than to believe someone like

Frayda. But then Flower Girl walked through the lawn and stood across the garden from Frayda. She stared at the radishes but made no move to pick them.

"When they're red like that and they pop out of the ground, it's time to pull them," Frayda said, which still wasn't really talking to Flower Girl; it was just, well, passing on some information. "My grandma says if you leave them in too long they just get hotter. And tough." When Flower Girl still didn't respond, Frayda squatted at the border of their garden, tugged a bunch of upright leaves, and revealed a huge round radish.

"Ready, all right," Flower Girl said, her feet planted at the opposite border across the garden.

Frayda saw the hose nearby, its nozzle leaking a little, so she decided to just walk over, rinse the radish, and hand it to Flower Girl. "Take a bite. I bet it's good. A little hot, maybe."

"No, you bite."

And so Frayda took a bite. "Umm. Pretty hot, like I said." As if that were all Flower Girl wanted to know, she turned without another word and hurried back to the row of chairs.

Now, since there was no pretending otherwise—she had

disobeyed her grandmother—Frayda decided that it couldn't make matters worse if she just knocked on the door to see if someone working inside could at least harvest the radishes. A young girl in a nursing uniform answered the door, listened to Frayda's advice, replied, "OK, thanks," and shut the door.

Nevertheless, as she changed for dinner, Frayda could see from her window the radish heads still in the ground. She thought she might tell her grandmother about her visit—which was almost an accident, really—but she knew it would only upset Nana Clara—and for no reason, really. Nothing had happened. So after dinner, before biking to the swim club to watch a diving meet, Frayda took no more than a few minutes and pulled thirty-nine radishes from the group home garden, rinsed them with the leaking hose, and placed them in a zippered bag, which she deposited on a chair by the door. Several of the Walkers saw Frayda, but no one came over or spoke to her. Even Flower Girl smoked in the background, though Frayda had hoped she would help.

The next day, instead of accompanying her grandmother to the nursery, Frayda staked and tied up the two dozen to-mato plants in their neighbors' garden. She found a sheet in her grandmother's rag bag, a faded, rose-patterned sheet

Frayda remembered sleeping on years ago; and this memory made her feel like a part-owner of the discarded cloth; and *that* permitted her to rip it into narrow bands. Since the cucumber seeds had sprouted, Frayda figured someone had better pull all but the sturdiest vine from each mound. (Nana Clara taught her that one uncrowded vine produces more than a tangle of crowded ones.) So that someone was Frayda. She was also the one to snap the large outer leaves from the butter-crunch lettuces that were about to bolt; she tucked them inside another plastic bag and placed the harvest on the orange chair. A man in the adjacent green chair, listening to a radio through his headphones, said, "Thank you," in a voice so loud that it startled Frayda, but she remembered how often she forgot to talk softly when she wore her Walkman.

But once again looking from her window before breakfast, Frayda saw the wilted lettuce leaves clinging to the flattened bag.

That weekend Frayda, Shawna, and Nana Clara drove to Cedar Point and stayed overnight at a nearby motel. Among

Frayda's souvenirs were 3-D postcards to send Gracie in Vermont:

We got to go on twenty-three rides (three different roller coasters), we swam in Lake Erie (kinda stinky), we visited a dinosaur park, and we did lots of other things that really wore out Nana Clara. Wish you could have come along.

As they drove through the alley to put Nana Clara's car in the garage, Frayda saw Flower Girl standing barefoot in the just-watered garden behind the blue Dumpster. As soon as her grandmother closed her bedroom door to nap after the long ride, Frayda raced over to the Walkers' home. Flower Girl was still watering, the hose clamped in her two hands like a snake she had wrestled into submission. "Been so dry lately," Flower Girl said. "I didn't see you today. Not yesterday, either."

"Hey, thanks," Frayda said, as if this were her own garden that Flower Girl had come to water. "You know, if you like flowers so much, how come this is the first time you've been over to garden?" Frayda used a very polite voice, because she didn't want her question to sound unkind. She stooped down and began to tamp the mud around the base of the tomato plants where Flower Girl's watering had washed it away.

"Can't use my hands, dear. Terrible arthritis, see? I can hardly hold this hose here, see? Used to, though. Used to have a garden, too. Not fancy like your grandmother's. Just a garden. Can't imagine everything she's got growing back there."

"Haven't you ever seen it all? It's amazing!"

"Nope. Don't think your grandmother likes me and my boyfriend."

Frayda tugged at some intruding tufts of grass, wondering what the right thing to say might be. *It's only because you steal her flowers? It's only because you pretend to have a boyfriend?* Finally, Frayda said, "Well, I think my grandmother thinks maybe some of the people here don't like *her* because, well, no one ever says hello back to her after she says hello."

"Christ almighty! Unless she shouted at the top of her lungs, half of us wouldn't even have heard her . . . We're not all deaf, exactly. Some are hard of listening because we're doing something else. And some are hard of seeing and some hard of lots of other things, too." This made Flower Girl laugh, which, in turn, made Frayda feel better about her answer.

"She didn't know that, I bet. I didn't know." Frayda stood up from behind the tomato plant where she'd been squatting, and said, "My name is Frayda. It's a little different, I guess: *F-R-A-Y-D-A*. What's yours?"

At first Flower Girl looked puzzled and Frayda thought that now, for sure, she'd said the wrong thing. *What if she doesn't remember her name?* Frayda thought. *Since she can hear and see all right, maybe forgetting is her problem.* But then, after a long pause, Flower Girl said, "Freida."

"No, it's pronounced Frayda, with a long *a* and then a short *a*."

"Your name's Frayda," Flower Girl repeated precisely, "and *my* name is Freida. With an *e* sound. Frayda. Freida. We have almost the same name...Frayda, Freida—"

Frayda extended her hand to shake. "And we both like gardens."

Freida reached for her hand, but then Frayda looked down

and realized how caked with mud her fingers were from working in the soil, and she withdrew her hand quickly, squatting again to rub her hands in the damp grass.

Unfortunately, before Frayda could even open her mouth to explain that rude gesture, Freida had headed toward the house as though she had tired of gardening altogether.

"Wait," Frayda called, but not at the top of her lungs.

Each day after swimming with Shawna or playing tennis or biking around Hawthorn Park, Frayda gardened alongside her grandmother, learning what Nana Clara called "horticultural tidbits": for instance, *To make a cauliflower nice and white, tie up the outer leaves around its head.* Some things that Frayda learned with Nana Clara, she'd try out the next time she had a chance to work in her adopted garden: *Always remove the suckers from the stems of the tomato plant;* or *Pluck the zucchinis just when the blossoms have fallen off the tips.* Whatever was ready to pick, Frayda delivered to the orange chair next to the kitchen door. Once in a while Flower Girl was there to say thank you and to take the vegetables inside. (Frayda was relieved that she had forgiven her for, or at least forgotten, that strange failed handshake.) The other days

Frayda just left the small harvest, hoping that someone would prepare the food and that someone would eat it.

The day before Labor Day, almost her last day in Ohio, Frayda bicycled home from the pool with Shawna to find Freida talking with Nana Clara at her front door.

"Uh-oh. Flower Girl's at your door! I bet your grandma caught her stealing flowers again!" Shawna guessed. "Look, she's even holding the evidence!"

It was true: Both of Freida's hands collared a bouquet of flowers ... the same coneflowers, bachelor's buttons, and cosmos that her grandmother had cut for a vase that morning. "Her name's Freida," Frayda replied. "Kind of like mine."

"Free-DUH? Free-*DU-UH!* She's Flower Girl."

"*Duh* yourself, Shaw-NUH! Why don't you get over all those stupid names of yours?" Frayda replied as she slid off her bike, leaving it flat, wheels spinning, in the middle of the drive.

"Oh, give me a break!" Shawna yelled.

"Did you have a good swim?" Nana Clara asked, pointing toward Frayda with the garden trowel in her hand. "Sweetheart, I want you to meet someone: This is Freida Donahue, she's one of our neighbors."

Freida buried her face in the blossoms of her bouquet, as if to hide—no, not hide but to inhale deeply.

"Hi, Freida," Frayda said.

"Hi, Frayda. Freida, Frayda. Freida. We both like gardens."

Nana Clara glanced back and forth between the two. "Well, no wonder Freida found my garden trowel in their garden this afternoon. I didn't know we had lost it."

"I didn't know we had, either—"

"Last night, by accident, you left it," Freida said. "But now it's back. So everything's OK."

"Well, thank you again for returning it," Nana Clara said, giving her granddaughter a look that was only partly a scowl. "I hope you both enjoy those flowers. We'll cut some more when that bouquet fades."

With that, Freida walked down the steps, carrying her bouquet in front of her like a heavy trophy.

Frayda tried to wedge past her grandmother, who expanded her arms to block the door. "I'm just going to run up and change, Nana," Frayda explained, but her grandmother didn't budge.

That was that. Frayda knew there was no pretending in-nocence. "Did Freida tell you—"

Nana Clara nodded yes.

"Did she say that I've—"

Nana Clara nodded yes again.

"Does this mean I'm in deep trouble? Grounded?"

Nana Clara held her head still for a long moment before she slowly shook it no, wrapped her arms around Frayda, and walked her into the house. "I asked you not to, you did anyway, so I would have a reason to ground you, right? But then, if you had told me what you were doing all these weeks, I would have told you not to, and...you know what? That also would have been wrong. More wrong, maybe."

"All I did was what *you* taught me from your garden," Frayda interrupted.

"Oy, so it's my fault after all!"

"It's just that their garden was going to waste."

"You know, when Freida first came to the door, my heart started up its loud beating, and I thought, *Now what, now what do I do?* And then she handed me my trowel and told me how you've been weeding and thinning and staking....

You know who I should be angry at? Me. You did what I or any of us on the block could have done, but no, we didn't. Instead you, my little summer volunteer, you did. If I could cut you a thank-you bouquet like I did for Freida, I'd have to chop down half my garden!"

Frayda hugged her grandmother and squeezed extra hard, sighing with relief.

Nana Clara said, "I guess you've been a volunteer like some of my plants, cropping up in a place I just didn't expect you belonged—and blooming even when I wasn't looking." Her grandmother kissed the top of her silky wet hair and then pushed Frayda's shoulders, rotating her toward the stairs. "Now go change out of your swimsuit—we've got plucking and tweaking to do for the block party tomorrow."

"Nana Clara?" Frayda called from the landing. "So when I'm gone, will you take over helping with their garden?"

"One last question, huh? Of course, yes is the answer. Your old grandmother will help, and I'll recruit some other volunteers. Now hurry and change!"

That night all the people around Hawthorn Park were busy making their specialty dishes. "Right now, I bet the

Dillons are marinating chicken wings," Nana Clara narrated, "the Crawford-Clouds are pulling taffy (there's never enough of *that* to go around), old Mrs. Reed is kneading her cloverleaf rolls—"

"What's Shawna's family cooking?"

"Oh, let's see. Her dad always brings his famous potato salad, which I think is famous for having too much mustard."

Frayda helped prepare Nana Clara's favorite end-of-summer block party dish—ratatouille, a weird French name that her grandmother sounded out for her, *rah-tah-too-ee*, umpteen times. First they harvested fistfuls of parsley and basil, then they gathered baskets of plum tomatoes, shiny eggplants, zucchini squash, and Spanish onions. Next they cut and chopped and peeled and sautéed, and finally they combined it all in a giant plastic container that barely fit in the rearranged refrigerator.

In the morning, after waffles spread with gooseberry jelly that Frayda had canned herself, the two of them did a little packing for Frayda's flight home the next morning. Frayda's mother phoned, as well: "I'll be there to pick you up, just like we planned, but we're driving on to Aunt Bebe's; we'll stay there a couple nights, since the painters still aren't done inside our house and all the furniture is hiding under drop cloths in the middle of the room. Then, unless your father wants—"

"Mom, that's fine, whatever is just fine," Frayda replied, trying not to be rude, but also trying not to think ahead to all the logistics of her Florida life.

At one o'clock, police barricades blocked the ends of Hawthorn Park. Picnic tables, folding tables and chairs, and lawn furniture all cluttered one side of the street. A few fathers talked beside the barbecue grills while the coals heated, and a few boys were already chasing one another along the street's new obstacle course. At two o'clock all the houses on the block were empty, covered dishes crowded the pushed-together tables, meats sizzled on the grills, kids raced around on Rollerblades, skateboards, bikes, and oversize scooter toys, and the old neighbors wandered from table to table, meeting out-of-town guests and smooching new babies.

Nana Clara and Frayda hopped in the food line with Shawna and her father. Everyone teased a sample of each dish onto a paper plate. "Just like you said, Nana Clara, there's enough food here to feed an army," Frayda said. "So where's the army? And where's—hey, look, there's Freida! And she's holding hands with—is that her boyfriend with her?"

"That's Baggie!" Shawna exclaimed, before her father glared at her.

"Look what we've brought," Freida announced, thrusting forward a plastic bag filled with cucumbers. "Twenty-one of them! All washed and ready to eat. And you can eat the skin, right, since there's no wax. And this is Evan. He's more shy than me, so don't mind if he just wants to eat."

Everyone nearby said hello to Evan (who didn't say hello back), and then Nana Clara made introductions all around.

Frayda cleared a little spot among the baskets and covered dishes. "Here, put them out on some paper plates."

Even before Nana Clara could return with a borrowed knife, Evan had produced a pocketknife and began to slice the cucumbers. "I harvested them myself. From *our* garden," Freida said. "Didn't even hurt my terrible arthritis. But Evan has to do the cutting, don't you, Evan?"

Evan answered by slicing: plate after plate of cucumber wheels, each one so perfect and thin that Frayda thought, just for a second, how they looked like wheels, wheels for some fairy-tale carriage that might carry off Flower Girl and her boyfriend. There were wheels enough for a dozen or a hundred carriages, enough for everyone in the group home, at the block party, in the whole—

"Here, you have the first slices," Freida said, interrupting her young friend's daydream.

Frayda forked a few cucumbers slices onto her plate, between Nana Clara's ratatouille and Shawna's father's too-mustardy potato salad. Her grandmother picked up one slice from her plate and ceremoniously nibbled the first sample.

Everyone watching leaned forward for her decision. "The best cucumbers I've ever tasted," she announced, as though her judgment weren't the least bit biased. "Better than any of my own! It must be—"

"It's on account of Frayda's green thumb," Freida proclaimed with a proud smile.

"Not her thumb," Nana Clara said, "on account of her green heart."

"Green heart?" Shawna mocked. "Are you suddenly, like, Irish?"

"Irish? I'm Irish," Freida announced, and continued to spoon out salads for herself and Evan. "So maybe we're related. Distant cousins, Frayda? Freida and Frayda, Freida and Frayda…"

"And we both like gardens," Frayda added.

The first day of class in yet another new school—this one in her just-built Florida home's neighborhood—Frayda drew a scene from her summer vacation. Each student had to stand in front of the room and tell about the drawing before pinning it to the bulletin board. Of course, Frayda drew a garden, an Ohio garden resplendent with every vegetable and fruit she could fit on one page, and with people, her Nana Clara and her— It was hard to explain, since this someone wasn't her half- or step- or even distant relation, this other woman with whom she had shared the season, plucking and tweaking. But what surprised even Frayda—what continues to surprise her today, so many summers later—is that when her teacher, Mr. Bancroft, said it was time to share pictures, Frayda, once again the new kid in the class, volunteered to go first.

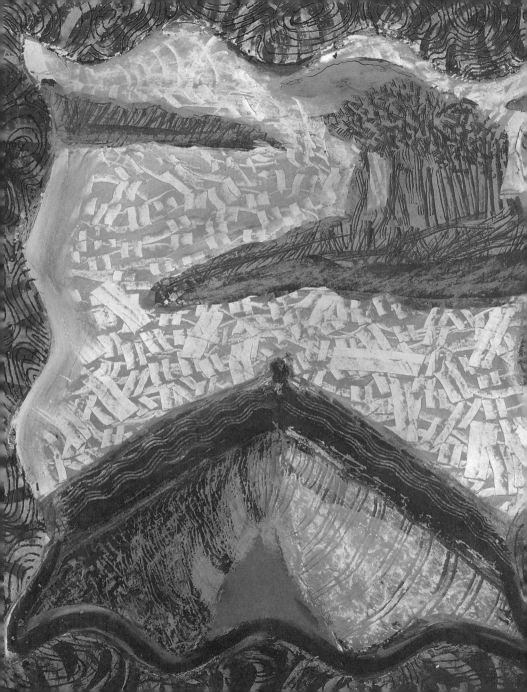

The Remembering Movies

SUNDAY, ON THE WAY BACK to Virginia from their beach house, where Decker had celebrated his eleventh birthday, his family stopped, as always, at Grandma and Grandpa Clifton's. "It's a movie of my birthday," Decker announced as he raced into the den to hug his grandmother, who was propped up on the couch, where he'd known she would be.

"Careful—the wiener dogs are hiding under here," she said, just as the blanket began to quake and Dwight and Delight, two dachshunds, burrowed out to add their greeting licks. "A movie! Oh, you and I haven't gone to the movies in so long! Remember, Decker, when you and I would go all by ourselves? Almost every Saturday when we weren't at the beach. Remember the Orpheum, downtown? And lunch at Woody's?"

"Sort of," Decker replied. "No, not really. Nessie, *gentle!* One *gentle* kiss for Grandma, that's it," Decker commanded, holding back their rambunctious Chesapeake Bay retriever.

"Grandma, cake, Grandma!" Hanna squealed in her highest just-turned-three-years-old voice, and paraded a paper plate with two slices of cake with a blue-icing crab and the word *Ha* scripted across the chocolate.

"Oh, birthday cake! And look, it has part of your name on it, Hanna! An *h* and an *a*," Grandma Clifton exclaimed.

"Nuh-uh, it's Decker's cake," Hanna insisted.

"Oh. Of course, that's the *Ha* part of *Happy,* silly me. *Ha-, Ha-, Ha-, Happy Birthday, Decker.*" Grandma laughed. "So tell me, who came to your party?"

"My friend Corey D'Amato gave me this," Decker said, and displayed his new wristwatch for his grandmother. "It has a stopwatch in it. I can use it for swim practice. And— you know how long I can hold my breath? Twenty-one-point-one seconds. Dad can hold his for fifty-one-point-three seconds. Grandma, hold your breath, I'll time you."

"Oh no, I'm too old. What if I can't start breathing again?"

"You will! Don't worry, just inhale a lot of air, pinch your nose, and close your mouth," Decker instructed.

"How about if you time how long it takes a grandma to give her grandson eleven birthday kisses," Grandma Rose countered.

"Too! Long!" Decker said, and squirmed out of her reach.

"Pop, find the remote control for the VCR," Decker's dad said. "We'll show you everyone at the party, that's better than telling!"

"What a birthday surprise for me! Now I'll get to go to your party after all," Grandma Rose said.

Decker's grandmother would never have missed the party, except she hadn't really left the house more than a dozen times in the past year, and those were only for doctors' appointments. She used to visit the beach each weekend, and when she and her husband were Decker's parents' age, she reared her two children there during the summer and every weekend—except the coldest ones—during the school year. How she loved those days with Grandpa Louie at the shore, although Grandpa Louie was mostly offshore, in one of his boats. She always said, "His department is getting fish. My department is cooking them. I'm needed on the boat like he's needed in the kitchen."

But other than fishing, Grandma Rose loved every aspect of beach life, especially when her children or her grand-children were there and she could indulge in all the things adults usually give up: searching for washed-up crab-pot floats, skipping stones, or collecting mummy chugs or softshell crabs that you could watch for an hour in a filled wash-basin. Grandma Rose knew how to braid oat grass into baskets, how to catch crabs off the dock by jigging a chicken neck on a piece of twine, and how to identify the sand tracks of many animals—muskrat, deer, killdeer, osprey. Even the humidity, the summer thunderstorms, and the garbage bag full of ale-wives that Grandpa stored in her freezer for baiting crab pots—she so loved that place, none of that seemed to matter.

But as she grew older, her memory clouded. Forgetting things seemed to make her tired, too, as though each lost memory or misplaced name were a little energy she no longer possessed. There were fewer and fewer days she felt up to the two-hour drive from their home in Virginia. They had never installed central air-conditioning in the beach house. Plus, without children, Grandma Rose began to feel bored there, since Grandpa Louie usually went fishing before dawn, either by himself or on Captain Tuttle's charter boat, to help tourists with their fishing rods. Once in a while Grandma agreed to visit the beach if her son's family—Decker and Hanna and their mother, Theresa—was having a special event, like a birthday. Her daughter, Diana, who lived in Manhattan, rarely traveled with her children on the train to Washington and then into the station wagon for the long ride to the bay.

About the time Decker entered fourth grade, Grandma Rose stopped visiting the beach altogether. Since then she spent her days in Grandpa Louie's old office, which he didn't need, having retired from his insurance business. In exchange her husband inherited the rest of the house: the kitchen, the laundry room, and all the other rooms, in which no one ever really did anything except vacuum (Decker always noticed the zigzag tracks on the carpet). "We've switched jobs," Grandma Rose kidded whenever anyone asked how her husband had taken to cooking. "Now he shops for shampoo and Sweet 'n Low, and I putter around the office and see my clients all day."

"Ah, if only *you* billed *your* clients," Grandpa Louie joked back.

The birthday tape flickered on the screen and then revealed a picture of the dock and all the chicken-wire crab pots stacked in three layers, a letter taped to each:

H A P P Y

B - D A Y

D E C K R

Stringers of lost and worn-out buoys that Grandma Rose herself had gathered over the years hung in swags from the boathouse and the dock posts—party-balloon size, and just as bright.

While Decker's father's recorded voice told his own version of the birthday party, his mother pointed out the party guests on the screen, supplying Grandma Rose with names. "So here are the Rogers kids and the Tillmans—there are five of them now: Charlene adopted two baby girls." Standing there explaining, she reminded Decker of Señora Perez, who came to school assemblies and translated them into Spanish for the new South American kids. "And here are Julia and Ted D'Amato from Alexandria—they met us at the beach—and their kids—"

"Now, who's that standing by the boat?" Grandma Rose asked.

"You know Mrs. Rogers!" Decker answered.

"Of course I know my neighbor of fourteen years. I'm just not used to seeing her in pictures!" Grandma explained to everyone. "She's cut her hair since I've seen her."

"Probably a dozen times, Mom," her son kidded. "And colored it, too!"

The video switched to a close-up of the grill and the rows of hot dogs and fish filets, and then to a colossal pot of corn on the cob, which steamed up the camera lens. Then Decker's father, who had shot most of the tape, surveyed all the people sitting around the picnic tables and on the dock benches and in the swing set, all balancing paper plates and soda cans. Everyone was supposed to offer Decker a special birthday wish "for posterity," but only the adults recorded messages. The kids made faces.

"Look at Mickey—he is so wacko," Decker said with pre-tend disgust, as he tapped the screen where a boy with a plastic spoon and fork hanging from his nose blew a kiss at the camera. *"Bappy Hirthday, Dicker."*

"That's an especially nice birthday wish, Mick," the televised father replied, barely able to keep from smirking, which caused Decker to fall into exaggerated laughter.

"Like the idea would never occur to you?" Decker's father turned to ask his son.

"Never," Decker said, and poked two fingers in his nose.

When the cake appeared on the screen, the candles shone brightly, because even though it was only eight o'clock, the shading trees that arched over the creek darkened the dock. And when the crowd in the movie began to sing the birthday song, Grandma and Grandpa Clifton started their own round, which made everyone but Decker join in.

"It took you nine-point-four seconds to sing 'Happy Birthday,' " Decker announced, holding up his official birthday timer. "I bet if you practice, you can do it in five."

The next shot—Decker opening his presents—did take place in the dark, but only because his father had forgotten to remove the lens cap when they moved to the beach house breezeway to escape the droves of mosquitoes.

"Grandpa...?" Grandma Rose spoke in a hinting voice and gestured toward the bookshelves.

"Oh yes, many happy returns," Grandpa Louie said as he reached up for a pair of envelopes. "For the birthday boy, and—look!—here's something for Hanna, too, because having you here is always an occasion we celebrate!"

After a round of thank-you kisses, Grandma Rose had several questions about the beach house. Besides, the tape had ended.

"Is that painting of you and Diana still hanging over the kids' bed?" she asked her son.

" 'Course, Mom. We haven't changed a thing."

"And what kind of curtains hang there? Did I ever..."

"The lace panel ones, remember?" Decker's mother supplied. "You ordered them from one of those catalogs you like so much. They have geese stitched at the bottom in an oval."

"No, honestly, I cannot remember them." Grandma Rose pouted. "Lace? Never mind."

"Well, I can't remember the name of that catalog... How's that for memory retention?" Decker's mother said.

"But I can't remember anything," Grandma Rose replied. "Nothing. My own house, where—"

"Well, when you're feeling a little better, we'll all go down for the afternoon," Grandpa suggested. "We can come back before dinner—and you'll see it all again."

"If and when I'm feeling better, I'll be able to remember *without* going there—excuse me, I think I'll make some coffee," Grandma said, and blotted her eyes with the edge of the blanket.

"I'll make it, Rose—don't get up," Grandpa Louie said.

Whenever Decker's family visited, his grandfather spent the time filling glasses with ice and soda, letting the three dogs in and out, arranging pillows behind his wife, and finding the newspaper clippings and magazine articles she had saved for someone. She usually had a whole folder of items for Decker: cartoons about soccer (which he had only played for one year, in fourth grade), catalogs of swimsuits or picture encyclopedias she'd requested for him, tips from *Reader's Digest* or some women's magazine about studying or eating well. And there were usually a few things about subjects, like parachuting, in which Decker had no interest.

"So why did she stick in these pictures of paratroopers?" Decker would ask his father.

"Well, at one point you talked about becoming a pilot someday, a paratrooper, even."

"Like, maybe when I was four or something," Decker would reply. "I don't remember saying that. Well, I don't want to now. Stuff like that really bugs me."

While Grandpa made everyone comfortable, Grandma did most of the talking—or asking, really. She had question after question, hardly waiting for one to be answered before posing another one. Decker suffered most of the questions, as though her memory were least strong regarding him. Hanna was really too little to answer many questions—and there wasn't that much about Hanna to even forget.

"What did you do at the beach, Decker?" "Catch many softshells?" "Did the Rogers get around to moving that rotting old boat?" "Decker, how old will you turn this summer?"

But she had to know the answers to some of her questions—such as, "How did you pick Nessie for the dog's name?"—which she asked Decker the evening of his eleventh birthday.

"Grandma, you named her!" Decker answered. "She was Nestlé because she's sort of chocolate, and then you called her the Loch Nestlé Monster that time she came in from swimming with all that seaweed on her back. We never call her Nestlé anymore."

"Of course I remember. I just couldn't think of it just then," she said. "Now you come sit beside me and ask *me* some questions."

Decker shoved the bunched blankets from the foot of the bed and plopped down. "I can't think of any right now."

On the ride home from his grandparents' house, Decker's mother and father discussed Grandma Rose's memory again. Every Sunday they talked about it as though she had changed—though Decker couldn't tell if it were for the better or for the worse.

"So is there anything she'll never forget?" Decker asked. Hanna had fallen asleep as soon as she had been buckled into the car seat. "How come she mostly forgets stuff about me? That doesn't seem very nice, does it?"

"Don't be silly, Decker. Actually, her doctors think that older memories, even things from her childhood, could be easier to recall. What's harder are recent events, names, everyday things. Even words like *fork* or *spoon* might become hard for her to say," Decker's father explained.

"*Fork?* She's going to forget the word *fork?* Even Hanna knows *fork.*"

"Maybe it will be some other thing, like the words for flowers or—"

"Will she still be able to use the silverware?" Decker asked. "She's not going to forget how to eat... and, like, stick the spoon up her nose!"

"Decker, we're having a serious discussion—," his father said.

"I'm being serious—"

"You're being a smart-ass, and I don't like it."

"You're supposed to say 'smart *aleck.*'"

"That's enough, Decker," his mother interrupted. "Understand?"

"Yes," Decker answered quietly. "So... will she still be able to feed herself if she can't say *fork*?"

Decker could suddenly hear the sound of tires on wet asphalt; it had been raining there.

"We've never asked that question," his mother finally replied, "but I think so. Sure. And sometimes words come back, too; if you remind her of something, she might remember again. For a while, at least."

"You mean, like, if Grandma went to the beach, she'd be able to remember stuff about it, like the curtains and Mrs. Rogers's name."

"We hope. She's young for being old, you know. She's not even seventy-five," Decker's father said.

"Why don't the doctors help her?" Decker asked.

"She's got a shelf of their medicines, but it takes time. I hope not too much time," his mother answered. "Decker, take the pillow and tuck it by Hanna's window so she can lean her head. And hand me the camera case so Nessie will stop pacing and lie down."

A moment later, Decker blurted out, "Will you show me how to really use the video camera?"

"Of course. If you'll be careful, which I know you will," his mother replied. "What for, all of a sudden?"

"I know what to do for Grandma! What if I make her a

video of the beach house? Next weekend. I'll shoot all the rooms and all the junk on the walls, and I'll walk down to her favorite beach, where she always used to take me, and then—and then she can watch the movie and remember more things."

"Now, that's being one good kid, Decker. Unbuckle your seat belt and let me give you a quick kiss," his mother said, reaching for her son. "Eleven years old, and there's still something I like about you."

"OK, Grandma, here we are driving into the driveway. It took us one hour, forty-one minutes, and twenty-two seconds to get here!"

"Decker, speak in your regular voice, the microphone picks up sound very easily," Decker's father coached.

"Yow! Sorry the picture's bumping, but you remember all the pits in the gravel. Dad, go slower."

"And you don't need to lean that far out the window with the camera." His mother tugged Decker by his back pocket.

"Here's a zoom-in picture of Mom telling me what not to do..."

"And here's your mom telling you not to show off for

your grandmother. Just be careful—stop taping for a minute." Decker's mother put her hand over the camera lens.

"Yow! Attack of the giant hand monster! Run, Grandma, run!"

"Decker, look at me. Don't act like a big shot just because you've got the camera. OK? Show Grandma...show her the new siding you helped put up."

"Big whup."

As soon as his father parked the van, Decker traced a complete circle around the beach house. Instead of joining his family for a swim, he spent an hour filming each part of the house—even the new siding. He zoomed into drawers and cupboards, recorded a panoramic view from each window, and surveyed the beachfront and boathouse as though he were inspecting the entire property for his grandmother, making certain that nothing was missing, nothing had been—or would be—forgotten. "And look, we have a bird's nest on the downspout. Zooming in...for a peek...Nope, the birds are gone. But there are still lots of osprey nests in the bay. Maybe Dad will let me take the camera on the boat."

Most of the weekend the video camera was near, if not in, Decker's hand. Whenever he thought something might interest his grandmother, he started filming. "Here's Mom in your favorite hammock," Decker narrated as he crawled beneath the suspended weaving to lie beneath the V of his mother's body. "Here's what the ants see when they look up and spot this net in the sky with a gigantic butt hanging over them."

"Decker...Just ignore him, Rose," his mother's voice interrupted.

"Oh no, the sky is falling, we'll all be crushed!" Decker squealed in his best ant voice.

The camera filmed a giant arm swatting underneath the hammock.

That evening Decker recorded his father restringing the archery bow that he'd had as a boy, when he'd been working on his scouting merit badge. With the birthday check from his grandparents, Decker had bought new targets, and his father filmed him practicing for his own archery merit badge. (Decker made his father erase the scenes of Decker missing not only the bull's-eye but the whole bale of hay that held the target.)

He waded out into the surf to film Hanna floating on their alligator raft with their mother. Decker even showed his newest best beach-friend Luke how to record, so he could feature himself in a long scene where he culled the keepers from the undersize crabs in the five crab pots they'd set the night before.

"Twenty-nine jimmies, twelve females, and twenty to throw back. Remember how to tell the jimmies from the females, Grandma? Luke, zoom in real close. The top button." Using the metal tongs, Decker held a crab up to the camera, and it promptly grabbed hold of the lens. "Jimmies have the Washington Monument on their belly shell, and females have the Capitol Building. See the dome on this girl?"

An hour before dusk, when the bluefish were sure to be biting in the bay, Decker asked his father if he could take pictures from the speedboat. "I'll be careful."

"You're welcome to, but your grandmother never so much as stepped on a boat. She'll probably snooze during the fishing scenes—"

"This part of the movie will be for Grandpa. He hardly ever gets to come out and fish with us since Grandma's been forgetting things."

"Let's hope we remember how to catch a few big ones."

"Dad! That's not something you forget," Decker said. "This will be the coolest. I can show us catching the fish, then you cleaning them, and then we can take them to Grandpa on the way home, and he can cook and eat the fish that he saw us catch!"

Everyone boarded the boat, including Nessie and Hanna, who didn't exactly improve the chances of catching fish. The speedboat cruised out of the creek into the no-wake zone and then soared into the bay, a crest of spray showering from the bow as the boat bounced over the waves.

"Shoot only once the boat has stopped," Decker's father shouted above the engine roar and the slapping waves. "And don't tell me you can't use the camcorder with the life jacket. It stays on."

Unfortunately, no school of bluefish ever crossed their path that evening, although Decker's dad maneuvered the boat through several of their usual fishing spots.

"OK, Grandpa, here's a close-up of the bloodworms," Decker narrated, "since that's the only thing we've caught so far. Well, really, we bought them at Buzzy's Baitstore. Buzzy said to tell you hi and that they all miss you. And here are some herring that Dad's cut up. But the bluefish must have gone out for Chinese food tonight. Remember, you used to say that? Nessie, get your nose away—"

But just as they were putting away the fishing lines, a trio of laughing gulls hovered overhead, and Decker passed the camera to his father. "Dad, get this on tape. Watch, Grandma. See if the gulls can catch the herring," he shouted as he tossed bits of fish into the air. This, of course, started Nessie barking and Hanna screaming to throw some pieces, too.

"He got one! Midair!" Decker called. "Did you record that, Dad?"

"Try to throw them out farther, Hanna," Decker's mother coached. "Want Mommy to help?"

"Quit laughing at us," Dad ordered the gulls. "We come out to fish and we end up throwing fish to the birds. It's a joke, and they get it!"

"Mom! Get Hanna out of the way, she's taking all the bait. Come on!"

A moment later Decker took the camera from his father. "OK, birds, we're out of herring," Decker called to the birds, who only continued to jeer.

For the last scene before dark, Decker filmed the sun setting right behind the beach house. His grandfather had always tried to bring the boat close enough to shore so that they could watch the orange sun—somehow it seemed bigger at sunset—sink among the pine trees along the creek, as though it belonged to them and returned to their boathouse after a long day of showing off in the sky. Sometimes Grandma Rose had brought a folding chair onto the beach and would be waving every so often at the other end of the orange path that the sun's reflection spread between her and the boat.

"Can you see the orange behind the house, Grandma? I don't know if the camera will show that."

"Sun, good night," Hanna called out.

The boat had drifted close enough so that Decker could see through the zooming lens of the camera (but not with his naked eye) the telescope in the bay window of the beach house. Grandma Rose used to stand with him there when he was little and she lived her summers at the beach, pointing out a bear, a swan named Cygnus, and even a pair of dogs in the heaven—"all of them right above our very own part of the bay," she would say. Even though Decker couldn't connect those star-dots to see those animals in that blackness, what he *could* always picture was his grandmother at the telescope, her arms around him, her one finger gently holding his eyelid shut as he squinted and blinked his eyelashes against the telescope's eyepiece and tried to call those creatures out of the dark.

The next evening Decker couldn't wait to show his new movie to his grandparents, even though he and Hanna had already watched it once at the beach. "Can't we see just a little of it before dinner?" he asked.

"Honey, it's sixty minutes long," Decker's mother answered. "And you were there!"

"All we're having is spaghetti and salad—let's eat in the TV room," Grandpa Louie suggested. "On TV tables!"

Amid the shuttling of paper plates, tables, and glasses, Grandpa continued, "When your father was little, we had a home movie camera. Oh, those old gadgets were impossible. You had to hold this heavy pair of floodlights above your head while you were filming—"

"And the lights were so bright," Decker's father continued, "that we are always squinting in the movies or holding our hands in front of our eyes to block the lights. You know, that's all I remember about the movies—I don't know what you ever recorded us doing besides squinting."

"Your growing up! You and Diana—," Grandpa replied.

"Decker? Did you hear that?" his mother asked him quietly. "See, we all forget." In a louder voice she suggested, "So we should transfer all those old reels onto a videotape so you and Diana can watch them. You'll be surprised at how much comes back."

"Well, good luck. They're buried in one of your mother's hundred shoe boxes in the basement," Grandpa Louie said. "Anyway, when your dad and Aunt Diana were little, we'd always set up TV tables to have TV dinners and watch TV! That was their idea of a perfect supper."

When Decker's movie began again on his grandparents' television, Decker instantly felt embarrassed. Or proud. Or plain weird. *It's strange,* Decker thought, *for a person to be watching something he's already done happening once again in a condensed version right on TV. In a room full of people watching him in the room and on the screen.*

Decker had filmed the last part only a few hours ago. This was like news—like an accident or a fire that was still happening somewhere in town and the TV station had rushed a camera crew to the scene and then back to the studio to air whatever they taped on the news. Decker had never really thought of his life as news (and, thankfully, he hadn't suffered an accident, except for the time he collided with the pool ladder and needed four stitches in his chin). But here was his weekend, a whole hour program on Channel 3. *Too weird,* he thought, *as soon as you put the tape into the VCR, you become someone else. You change from a "me" into a "him." You're no longer the guy in the movie or making the movie, you're the guy watching the movie at home: There is Decker who holds the camera and narrates, and there is Decker in his grandparents' house, with a forkful of spaghetti, who watches the television.*

As Decker watched himself, or even the other people he had recorded, he often knew exactly what was going to be said. He could remember whole sentences, word after word, without even having tried to remember them—without even wanting to!

"Wait, watch this. You'll love this part, Grandma," Decker announced as the scene changed and his mother's blurred shape in the hammock grew distinct. "Here comes the ant's-eye view."

"That's because Decker always has ants in his pants," his mother said.

And when the ants squealed, *"The sky is falling!"* Decker and Hanna both squealed along with the TV, adding to the chorus of ants.

Everyone laughed so hard Grandma pushed the rewind button, and they watched the scene two more times with everyone squealing, "The sky is falling!"

Later in the movie, when the gulls squawked above the boat and Hanna shrieked with joy and Nessie perched on the deck barking, the TV room filled with even more noise: six people talking and laughing, Hanna clapping, Nessie howling, and even the added yips of Dwight and Delight.

But when the picture changed to the sunset over the beach house, the room fell quiet and Grandma Rose said, "This was the perfect way to spend a beach weekend."

"Did you see lots of stuff you forgot, Grandma?" Decker asked. "So you can remember it now?"

"Decker, you showed me things I'd never even seen before

and never had the chance to forget. And I did it right here from my couch."

"You can't imagine how hard Decker worked on this, Mom," his father said. "He did everything but record while he was asleep."

"Great idea, Dad," Decker said. "Next weekend you stay up all night and film me while I'm dreaming."

"Grandpa, before they go, don't forget our little surprise," Grandma said.

"What surprise?" he asked.

"Don't forget to give Decker the envelope. And don't we have something for Hanna, too?" Grandma whispered.

Grandpa walked over to his wife and replied, tentatively, "What envelope, honey?"

"The birthday cards," she said. "*You* remember."

"You gave me my birthday money card *last* Sunday, on my birthday," said Decker.

"Last week? But if your birthday is— Oh yes, of course. But you know how grandmas love birthdays," Grandma said.

"Mom, we've tired you out with all this commotion— we should be heading off," Decker's father said. "OK, good-bye hugs for everybody. Hanna? Decker?"

"But it was even in the movie: We already bought my new archery targets with their—," Decker added.

"Then you should thank them, Decker," his mother prompted.

"Will there be another movie sometime soon, my big man?" Grandma Rose asked as she reached for her hug.

"Another movie? What about?" Decker gave the dachshunds kisses on their heads, too. "Bye, Dee-light; bye, Dee-wight."

"About you. About my Hanna. About anything I'm missing!"

"OK, if I can think of something."

"What's to think about? I'll love anything. Anything. Just promise me another one," said Grandma Rose. "You'll be my vacation. I'll go along with you, anywhere you want to go, and I'll watch just what you see."

"OK, I promise," Decker said as he shrugged. "Thanks again for the archery stuff."

As Grandpa escorted everyone to the garage, Grandma called, "Don't forget!" though Decker didn't know if she meant for Grandpa not to forget the birthday envelopes or for Decker not to forget his promise.

————

"Decker, you're old enough to understand this," Decker's father said once they'd waved their last good-byes to Grandpa Louie at the bend in the driveway. "When your grandmother forgets something and you remind her that she forgot, it makes her feel worse. More confused."

"So what am I supposed to do, pretend it's my birthday every time she says it is?"

"Well, in this case—," Decker's mother fumbled.

"All I did was tell the truth, which is what you say I'm supposed to do—"

"Can I finish? Maybe letting her believe that something's true isn't the worst thing in the world—"

"So now you're saying—"

"Are you honestly angry, Decker?" his father interjected. "Because if you're just frustrated and worried along with the rest of us, then you can find another way of expressing it. It's not like *you* are having this hard growing-old problem. Your grandmother is, and it's difficult for everyone—especially your grandfather, and you don't see him losing his patience."

"He probably does when we're not there," Decker

quipped. "Why isn't she better? She has all those pills and doctors! My birthday was just last week, and she remembers everything else fine, doesn't she—"

"No, she doesn't," his father explained. "The doctors can't say why. She gets disoriented. Especially when she's tired, I think. Do not take it personally. And certainly don't get angry at Grandma."

"I wasn't angry. Just forget it. OK? Forget it."

"No, we can't 'forget it,'" his father insisted. "I wish we could forget it, because that would mean your grandmother would stop forgetting, but she can't."

Decker's mother added, "Just try to overlook Grandma's small mistakes."

"I already said *OK*. Can we drop it?" Decker asked. "How about stopping for root beer floats on the way home?"

"Floats-floats-floats!" Hanna awakened to chant excitedly, which meant the answer was no longer going to be no.

Every week after his birthday, Decker worked on new tapes for *Sunday Night at the Movies* at his grandparents' house, where they would have dinner on their way home from the beach.

When he wasn't at swim team practice, or mowing lawns with his summer business partner, Johnny Lee, or hanging out with his friends, Decker carried the camera in his backpack. He even convinced his parents to buy a second battery, so one could always be recharging.

During the Fourth of July weekend, when his family visited Aunt Diana and her children in New York City, Decker recorded two hour-long tapes, including a ferry boat ride that looped them around the whole island of Manhattan. *"Here's Ellis Island, Grandma,"* Decker pointed out, and he could see his blurred finger at the end of his arm pointing toward the island as if he had discovered land. *"Here's where your mom and dad landed in America with you and Samuel, Dad says. But you were too little to remember."*

During a week of tennis camp, Decker let his mom make most of the tennis movie so he could be in it. It was a problem, being both the cameraman and the main star.

Another week, Decker made a movie called *Hanna's Holiday.* It was just a regular day in his sister's life, but the word *holiday* sounded better than just plain *day* in the title: Hanna dancing in front of the television. Hanna dumping out two of her toy bins. Hanna spilling apple juice. *("If you like this part, I can make a whole movie just of Hanna spilling stuff, Grandma.")* Hanna dancing with her friend Tina in a plastic pool on Tina's deck. Hanna making thumbprint cookies with their mother to take to Grandma and Grandpa's that very Sunday.

"You know what would be awesome, Mom?" Decker exclaimed at the table as he finished shooting Hanna with a mashed-potato beard. "You can help me make signs on the computer. And I can shoot them so I can have credits! You know, at the end of the movie: *Starring Hanna Clifton as the little girl, Tina Rodriguez as the little girl's best friend. Director: Decker Clifton. Narrator: Decker Clifton.*"

" '*Egomaniac: Decker Clifton,*' " his father added.

"What's the egomaniac do, Dad? Is he, like, the makeup guy?"

"Your father's kidding you, Decker," his mother replied. "An egomaniac is a person who thinks too much of himself. No, your idea's great; we'll try it after we clean up. Hanna, let's wipe your face."

"I was going to give you credit, too, Dad. You and Mom

were going to be the producers. Aren't they the ones who pay for everything, like the film and the equipment and the actors' salaries?"

"Gee, thanks," Decker's dad replied. "Hanna, what do I owe you for working today?"

"Peas more apple juice."

In August Decker recorded one movie of their Chesapeake Bay retriever's entire morning walk; a tape of a swim meet where Decker's team lost most of the races but Decker himself won two second-place ribbons, for a relay and for his backstroke; a tape of a bike trip his scout troop took to Annapolis; and one last summer-vacation tape, of their day trip to Chincoteague to see the island's wild horses.

By the time school commenced, Decker had become a very accomplished cameraman—he'd made two dozen movies. "You can operate that thing better than I can," his father admitted. Decker could zoom in smoothly, pan a scene without blurring, and even review his tape while it was in the camera in order to decide if he wanted to shoot a retake.

"I'd need exactly one whole day to watch all my remembering movies," Grandma Rose told Decker the Sunday before school began. "Twenty-four tapes, twenty-four hours. So many things to remember. And all in one place—besides my head!"

After dinner, the movie, and a long good-bye, Grandma Rose called out to her husband, where he was ushering everyone out the garage door. "Grandpa, get Decker and Hanna some of that black licorice from the candy jar. They always like that when we have it."

"Oh, I must have forgotten to buy some," Grandpa Louie confessed, shaking his head no very slowly, to show his grandson that he knew what Decker was thinking.

"That's OK, Grandpa," Decker whispered. "Me and Hanna don't like licorice."

As Decker's family walked in the door of their own house, Grandpa Louie's voice was leaving a message on their answering machine: "*. . . so I'll drive your camera over sometime this week.*"

"Shoot! We left the camcorder there!" Decker exclaimed, and snatched the phone. "Grandpa, we're here, we're here."

"Tell him we don't want him driving all this way; we'll get it next Sunday," Decker's father said.

"Gramps, Dad says— Wait!" Decker covered the mouth-piece with his hand. "We have to get it! We won't have a new movie to show Grandma!"

"I could hear that," Grandpa said. "She'll be fine without a new movie next Sunday. We can just show her one of the old ones; you know your grandmother . . . she won't know the difference. It's the visiting that's—"

"What do you mean, Grandma can't tell? They're all different. She's remembering things when she watches—she says they help—"

Decker's father took the phone. "Decker, can you help your mom unpack the cooler?"

"But he said Grandma doesn't even know—"

"Decker, I need your help," his mother yelled on cue from behind the refrigerator's open door.

In a moment, his father joined the two of them trying to jam the extra milk jug and the sack of steamed crabs into the packed shelves.

"Kiddo, I don't want you to be upset. I know you're doing your best to understand, but maybe Grandma's memory won't get better. Even with all her pills and doctors. She could get worse. We need to think about that."

"She can't even tell if she's watching a movie she's already seen? A stupid home movie?" Decker argued.

"I know you put so much time into your movies, and Grandpa didn't mean to hurt your feelings, but I don't think anyone knows how much your grandmother does understand or remember—"

"Then why do we even have to go visit? Does she even remember if we've visited or not?"

"Decker, she loves to see you and Hanna each week—you can tell that," his father replied.

"But honestly," his mother added, "Grandpa says some Mondays she doesn't remember our visiting, and you know we haven't missed a Sunday in months. But still, you see how she loves watching your movies... and so what if she doesn't remember it all later?"

"So what? So *what*? So who cares if I make her movies or not?" Decker said in a voice that could have been angry if it weren't so sad.

"Or think of it this way," his father reasoned. "If she did remember them all, then maybe she wouldn't want to watch them again, but Grandpa says she watches your movies over and over, all the time."

Decker thought about that and then replied, "Is she going to forget my name, like how she didn't even recognize Cousin Lenny's name and Paul's name when they went to visit?"

"Come sit at the table, Decker," his father said. "Look, she might forget your name someday—she's called me *her* father's name a few times—so maybe you'll have to overlook that, too. But she still loves you, even if she calls you another name for a moment. And even if she is confused, you're not. You love her, right? You're not going to forget that, even when—"

"Even when, like, one day she thinks I'm just some kid—like the paperboy or the kid who shovels the snow?" Decker pulled the empty camera case from his backpack and fiddled with the straps.

"Decker, this is our problem, and we're all going to share it along with Grandma," his mother said. "But your father's right: Even if she forgets things, or can't appreciate your movies, or calls you by a different name, you still have your memory, don't you? Don't you?"

"Yes. So what?"

"Well, you'll remember that she's your grandmother and

you're her very first grandchild, who she loves more than anything in the world. You'll always have wonderful memories of her."

"I don't know. It's hard," Decker said, reaching into the empty camera case as though it held some answer.

Then Decker's father said, in a voice that was so calm it seemed he had forgotten how sick his own mother had become, "Do you know how lucky you are? Think of Hanna. She never really knew the Grandma Rose you knew, and if we lose Grandma soon, or even years from now, Hanna probably won't even remember Grandma when she was well. Maybe she won't remember much about her at all."

"Hanna? But Hanna's little. Her remembering isn't sick," Decker answered.

"Honey, we all forget things," his mother said. "We all just forgot the camcorder, remember? And you don't remember when we lived in the apartments in Alexandria, until you were two. Or going downtown to the Orpheum and to Woody's with Grandma. But Grandma remembers. And Dad doesn't remember the old movies Grandpa took of him and Aunt Diana. Early memories vanish pretty quickly. And

Hanna's will, too. But other people can remember for you. And remind you, sometimes."

"You know, Decker," his father said, "maybe what your movies are supposed to show Grandma has nothing to do with helping her remember. Nothing even to do with what you've recorded, what you've seen, or done, or places you've been."

"Then what's the use?" Decker asked.

"Maybe all the movies are supposed to show is that you love her. Even a grandmother who forgets can see that."

For a long moment, Decker looked anywhere except at his parents. "What if one day I'm old and forgetting like Grandma, Dad?"

"What if one day your Mom and I are old and forgetting?" Decker's father took his mother's hand. "It could happen to us first. I wish I could tell you I know the answer, and that I know the answer is no, it won't happen. But who can predict those things, Decker? We just have to live right now and make sure that whoever we love knows it. No matter what. No matter what they're going through."

Decker aimed the camera case at his father and pretended

to zoom in until he could see the little bit of water at the edge of his father's eyelids.

Decker wished he could have filmed his first day of sixth grade, not only for his grandmother but because the camera would have made it easier to meet some of the new kids. But when his family arrived at his grandparents' house after their beach weekend, they brought only cold steamed crabs and a peach pie. Grandma felt strong enough to join them at the newspaper-covered kitchen table, and they all answered her questions as they cracked and peeled crabs to pluck tidbits of meat from the shells.

"Who made that most delicious pie?" Grandma Rose asked for a second time, and for a second time Decker answered. "Me and Mom and Hanna. But Hanna didn't do anything but smush her hands in the dough."

Decker had questions of his own. "Grandma, which of my movies is your favorite one?"

"Oh, I love them all the most," she answered. "They're my favorite movies of all time, and you know how I liked to go to movies."

"No, really. Like, do you remember the one about my swim team?"

"Decker, you may *not* quiz your grandmother," his father ordered.

"I don't know. Which one do you mean?" Grandma replied hesitantly.

"See!" Decker fired back to his father, his mouth fixed in a frown. "It doesn't matter."

"You're excused, young man," his father said. "You may wait in the car."

"It's all right," Grandpa offered.

"You mean the one where I see you win the race at the pool?" his grandmother continued, even before Decker could scoot his chair from the table. "Or do you mean the one where you're standing in front of your bulletin board with all your ribbons? My champion swimmer!"

"Oh. I guess there *are* two of them," Decker replied, unsettled by her response.

"Go ahead, answer your grandmother," Decker's father said. "You may stay."

"I guess the one at the pool."

"Well, you're the best swimmer on the team, that I can judge from my couch!" Grandma Rose replied.

Decker tried another question. "Do you like the movie that I took at the—"

"I love them all!" Grandma Rose answered enthusiastically. "The one of Nessie chasing the seagull and the one with Hanna and her potato beard and the ones with your friends Jeffrey and Kenzie and the kids from the school you go to—shoot! I can't say the name of it..."

"Pfeiffer Forest Elementary School—it's a hard name to remember. Or spell," Decker answered.

"See," his father said, and stood to kiss the top of Decker's head, and whispered, "she might remember lots more than we know."

"And this pie! Did you make it, Theresa?" Grandma asked as she lifted the last bite to her lips. "It's those Hale Harrison peaches that make the best pies."

"Who's Hale Harrison?" Decker asked, but no one knew the answer.

Just as everyone was finishing the cleaning (Decker decided his job was sneaking the dogs bits of crabmeat from

Hanna's plate), Grandma called from her den, "It's time for *Sunday Night at the Movies.*"

"Movies, movies. My movie!" Hanna chanted.

"Dad, we have to go. I have homework," Decker said, mouthing the words *I don't want to watch* for his father to lip-read.

"This won't take long, Decker. We can watch a little."

"But we didn't bring anything new—I don't want to pretend—"

"Don't worry," Grandpa Louie said to Decker. "Tonight you're invited to *our* world premiere."

Everyone gathered in the den and Grandma Rose pressed the play button on the remote control. But instead of Decker's voice and instead of the screen showing a school or a beach or a swimming pool, a picture of the very den where they were all sitting appeared on the television, as though they were all being recorded, right at that moment in their lives together. Then the voice of Grandma Rose announced, *"Now that I have the camera, I get to make a movie for you. See, if I hold the camera, no one can see that I haven't done my makeup and hair. So, no, Grandpa, you can't be the cameraman. You'll just have to show me how to work it."* The screen revealed a picture of the two dachshunds sniffing at the camera lens. *"Maybe if the wiener dogs are good, I'll let them shoot some pictures of squirrels a little later. And here comes my first guest star: Grandpa in his famous role as Chef Clifton. Yum. Breakfast."* The camera swept across the room to Grandpa (most of him, at least, since Grandma had cut off the top of his head), who carried in a tray with juice, oatmeal, a glass of pills, and dog biscuits. *"One for you and one for you and a few for me,"* the televised grandmother said, placing a biscuit in each of the dachshund's mouths and tossing the pills into her own (that's when the room turned sideways—Grandma Rose must have laid the camera on its side to wash down the pills).

"Look, in the background: It's my movie about Hanna's day," Decker said, and tapped on the TV at the recorded version of the TV in the background.

Grandma's movie panned the room and the window where the sun rose between the pollonia trees. *"You know those are my favorite trees in the universe. We planted them exactly forty years ago, when we built this house."* After a few frames of her ankles and the blankets, the taped grandmother announced, *"And here comes your Aunt Sylvia with a whole collection of magazines. I don't subscribe to anything because she brings me hers each week."*

Grandma Rose had filmed the dachshunds eating their kibble, Grandpa refilling the dachshund-shaped salt and pepper shakers, the sunset behind the sliding glass doors in the den, Grandpa drying off Dwight and Delight's feet from the rain. But most of the movie was Grandma narrating the items that lined the shelves of her den, the artwork on the refrigerator, and the photographs on the nightstand in her upstairs bedroom, where Decker couldn't recall visiting. Everything was Decker's and Hanna's.

"Here's the calendar that you made me on the school computer. And my Mother's Day present of your hands pressed in the clay. But your hands wouldn't fit in there now, would they? Oh, and here are paintings—where did you make these? school?—you know, with the leaves and the potato stamps. Here are a few of your cousin... your cousin's drawings. They don't send me so many since they always get wrinkled in the mail. And over here—move out of the way, Dwightness—over here is Hanna's whole body cutout that she colored at day care. She's such a big girl now, but I like to look over and see that silhouette on the door and pretend that she's coming in to visit."

Decker stood up and pointed to each thing in the den that his grandmother had filmed for her movie. He held up the Popsicle-stick candy dish he'd made in scouts and pretended to be one of the models on a game show as his grandmother described it on the screen.

"Hey, look now," Decker said. "There's another movie in the background—the one I took in New York!"

"It seems like her whole movie is about you—you and Hanna," Decker's father whispered.

The grandmother on the tape and the grandmother in the room continued their narration, one telling about her day and the other telling about the movie of her day. "Decker, how can you hold the camera up so long? It gets heavy. That's why I have so much stopping and starting..."

"So here I am after a little snooze—whenever the dogs nap, I feel like I should keep them company. Their favorite remembering movie is the Nessie one, though they've never been to the beach. They think the only wieners that belong at the beach should go in hot-dog buns. I bet you the waves would scare them."

After a few seconds of blank screen (Grandma Rose had probably forgotten to take off the lens cap), she announced,

"And look who's come to visit! It's Mrs. Feinstein. Say hello to my grandchildren."

While everyone continued watching the movie, Decker picked up the video camera, loaded it with a blank tape from his backpack, and began to record. "It's *Sunday Night at the Movies,*" he narrated, "watching *Sunday Night at the Movies.* And here's the star of our show, Rose Clifton, also known as Grandma!"

"Wait a second, Mr. Director! You're not making a movie of me. I don't want to be in the movie. I want you and Hanna."

"But now I have the camera back, and I want a movie of you!" Decker joked.

"Remembering movies are for old ladies, not young boys! You're so silly," Grandma Rose replied.

Decker's father said, "You can sit still for a little taping, Mom. Don't worry, you did your makeup. You look like a movie star."

"And here is Grandma's favorite program of the week: *Sunday Night at the Movies,*" Decker spoke in a loud newscaster's voice. He brought the camera close to the television and re-recorded the image that his grandmother had filmed sometime that week, as though his movie were remembering her movie. Through the eyepiece, Decker saw a picture of himself on the television—his first-grade school picture in a tin frame on the kitchen windowsill. He retaped his grandmother's voice saying, *"I'll never forget what you wrote on the back of the picture: 'For Grandma Rose, my favorite flower.'"*

"It's my favorite program—not just on Sundays. Every night of the week!" Grandma Rose added. "And every morning. It's my *Good Morning Show* and my *Late Night News* and my *Noontime News Hour* and my—Grandpa, what's the program where the news people broadcast some place new every day?"

"*Live at Five,*" Grandpa answered. "It's true: She made me cancel our cable TV."

"Who needs it, now that I have a whole station devoted to my grandchildren? It's every grandparent's dream. Now what about pie?" Grandma asked, and pointed into Decker's lens as though he were in charge of dessert. "Someone said we were having pie."

Decker zoomed the camera lens toward his grandmother's face until the tiny frame before his eye held only her eyes and her nose. "We *had* dessert—I mean, last week we had a great dessert," Decker corrected himself, "and this week we're having pie, Grandma, as soon as your movie's over."

"My movie? I'm done with my movie," Grandma Rose said. "You tape over that one and make me a new one for next week. I was just fooling around to surprise you. Weren't you surprised?"

Decker didn't answer that question, but he knew he'd never erase Grandma Rose's movie.

In fact, each Sunday when Decker and his family came to visit, whether or not he had made his grandmother a new movie, Decker filmed a few scenes on that same tape of his Grandma Rose for his own remembering movie—and for Hanna, too, who might not remember. That way, if years from then Grandma Rose forgot more and more—like how to work the remote control, the color of the beach house, the name of the swan constellation or her favorite kind of peach or even the name of her first grandchild—Decker would be able to slip his tape into the VCR and watch his grandmother remembering all the people and places and things that, even without a name, she loved.

Acknowledgments

These stories, written over several years, have many debts that publication will hardly repay in full. Nonetheless, a few words of gratitude are set here for the record.

"The Remembering Movies" owes an inestimable thanks to Shirley and John Gasper and their family, in which my own has been so welcome. The character of Matthew in "The Trust of a Dolphin" derives, in part, from my many years of friendship with David Hameroff, and the dolphins themselves reflect information I gathered from the staff at Dolphins Plus; I have both Brenda Peterson and Erich Hoyt to thank for their encouragement of this story. "Mastering the

Art" is dedicated to Tom Wharton. The cover and interior illustrations realize, in some small way, a dream that Matthew Valiquette and I have shared for decades. Finally, I hope that, bound within this book, is something of the unbounded love I have for three people: Mark, who shares each story even before it's been drafted on a page; Mimi, who continues to read and shape each word I've written; and Liz, who turns each part of bookmaking into the heart's own art.